PIRATESHIP DOWN

Stories from the world of
The Sentinels of New Orleans

SUZANNE JOHNSON

PIRATESHIP DOWN: Stories from the World of the Sentinels of New Orleans/Suzanne Johnson—1st edition
ISBN 978-0-9968220-0-8

Cover design by Robin Ludwig Design, www.gobookcoverdesign.com
Interior Design by Woven Red Author Services, www.WovenRed.ca

Other Books by Suzanne Johnson/Susannah Sandlin

Writing as Suzanne Johnson

The Sentinels of New Orleans Series (Urban Fantasy)
Royal Street
River Road
Elysian Fields
Pirate's Alley
Belle Chasse (2016)

Christmas in Dogtown

Anthologies
Dark Secrets: A Paranormal Noir Anthology
containing the novella, *The Consort*

Writing as Susannah Sandlin

The Penton Legacy Series (Paranormal Romance)
Redemption
Absolution
Omega
Allegiance
Illumination (2016)

Storm Force (Paranormal Romance)

Chenoire (Paranormal Romance)

The Collectors Series (Romantic Suspense)
Lovely, Dark, and Deep
Deadly, Calm, and Cold

The Wildlife Wardens Series (Romantic Suspense)
Wild Man's Bluff (2016)

Table of Contents

* In New Orleans, lagniappe means "a little something extra."

Dedication

To NOLA, past and present and forever.

Foreword

Welcome to the Sentinels multiverse! Haven't read any of the series? No worries. The stories in this volume lie outside the main arc of the Sentinels of New Orleans series. For those of you who fret over such things, however, you'll find an introduction to each story that tells you where it would fall in the grand scheme of things.

All you need to know is that the Sentinels world revolves around New Orleans and South Louisiana, where many preternatural species are maneuvering for power among the unsuspecting humans. In this volume, you'll read about wizards and mermen, an undead French pirate and shapeshifters—heavy on the undead French pirate.

In 2005, I was a happy New Orleanian, working as an editor at Tulane University. Late that summer, Hurricane Katrina changed everything, including what I wanted to do with my time. That I'm here years later, having grown to love a world and a family of characters that sprang from chaos and loss, is both a revelation and a blessing. If you've been with me on this journey, I offer a humble thank you. If you're new to this world, I offer a heartfelt welcome.

Within these pages (whether physical or virtual), you'll find a new novella, *Pirateship Down* , plus other stories that have appeared for limited online runs over the past three years. All have been updated for this edition.

Get ready for lively urban fantasy, a heavy dose of South Louisiana culture, a few laughs, and did I mention mermen and pirates? As we say way down in New Orleans: yeah, you right.

TALK LIKE A PIRATE

"Talk Like a Pirate" was originally published in a shorter form as a free read on my website, and it offers a rare chance to see the undead early 19th-century French pirate Jean Lafitte and New Orleans wizard sentinel (i.e., border guard) Gerry St. Simon as they interacted before the start of the series. When the pirate Lafitte appears in the first scene of Royal Street, *the first book in the series, we're told that the crafty Frenchman has long had a habit of popping into modern New Orleans from his home in the otherworld, the Beyond. The character of DJ Jaco does not appear in this short story.*

For those interested in timelines, this story takes place in New Orleans and in the St. Charles Parish community of Destrehan, Louisiana, about one or two years prior to the events of Royal Street.

One

I HUNCHED OVER MY plate and pretended not to know my roommate.

"Arrr, Matey, ask me who it is." Megan leaned across the counter with a squinched eye and skewed mouth, trying to look like a pirate chick. She failed.

All she accomplished was earning us a few stares from the combination of business people, tourists, and students stuffing down omelets at the Camellia Grill in New Orleans' Riverbend neighborhood.

"I don't care," I told her. "Eat your breakfast."

She ignored me. "Ask me who my guest is, Rhyn me girl, or I'll lash ye to the mast."

Meg hadn't shut up about Talk Like a Pirate Day for the last month, planning her big party and teasing her friends with the promise of an unforgettable special guest. I didn't do pirates. Unless Orlando Bloom showed up with a five-day stubble, a vintage costume, and a nametag that read *Will Turner*, I didn't care who her special guest was.

The New Orleans streetcars rumbled on the tracks behind

3

us, and an occasional ship's horn bellowed from the Mississippi River a block away. Middle-aged servers and cooks in crisp white shirts and bow ties shouted to each other and bantered with customers across the counter as they flipped eggs, fried bacon, and poured coffee.

"I'm not going to beg you to tell me who your guest is." I downed my last bite of cheesy omelet and dabbed at my mouth with a napkin. "If you want to tell me, tell me. Otherwise, I've got a finance test next Wednesday and that's my priority."

I'd put finance off till my last semester of grad school and time had run out. No finance, no MBA. I hated every single second of it.

"Pffft." Meg grabbed both checks and slid off her stool. "It's only Friday. Party's on Sunday. That gives you plenty of time to study."

I shook my head and let Meg pay for breakfast. She could afford it. Scoffing at grad school, she'd gone straight to work after finishing at Tulane last year. She put her art degree to work designing floats at Mardi Gras World while I tried to understand the complexities of corporate finance.

We walked to the corner and waited for the streetcar. Meg was in a pout, hands stuffed in the pockets of her jeans.

God save me from the roommate guilt trip. "Okay, tell me about the special guest."

She feigned indifference for about three seconds before caving. "Remember I told you I'd been experimenting with"— her voice dipped to a stage whisper—"my gifts?"

4

Ugh. Meg fancied herself a witch or warlock or some other kind of magic-wielding headcase. I'd never seen anything from her more special than a good sense of intuition.

"Yeah, so?"

"So, I've figured out a way to summon Jean Lafitte. I mean the *real* Jean Lafitte, not an impersonator. Just think—New Orleans' most famous pirate at our party!"

"*Your* party." I groaned inwardly. She'd gone insane, and her family lived in Massachusetts. That left only me to call the little men in white coats and have her committed. If the little men wore bad pirate suits beneath those white coats, she might go without a fight.

"Meg." I kept my voice reasonable, as if this weren't the most ridiculous conversation in the history of the world. "Jean Lafitte has been dead for at least two hundred years." Arguably New Orleans' most infamous citizen in the city's long history of infamy, Lafitte had torn up the waters of South Louisiana and the Gulf Coast before the War of 1812, if I remembered my history lessons.

"And he was a real pirate," I reminded her. "He wouldn't pop out of a cake and hand out party favors. Lafitte, like, *killed* people."

"Nonsense." She waved me off, climbing the steps into the streetcar and dropping her coins in the box beside the driver. "That was just bad PR."

I slid in the seat next to her. "Bad PR? Well, jeez, too bad Jean Lafitte couldn't hire a decent publicist."

"Hey, I've read up on him, okay? He was the *gentleman* pirate. Really smart. He had pirate flunkies to do all the dirty work while he romanced the ladies and played poker."

We swayed as the streetcar made its sharp turn from Carrollton onto St. Charles Avenue and rumbled toward Tulane. "Great. He won't kill you himself. He'll just order someone else to do it."

Why was I arguing with her? It's not like she could really summon Jean Lafitte.

Two

AT FIVE UNTIL MIDNIGHT, I sat at the kitchen table eating chips and drinking a bottle of Abita Amber. A used copy of *Applied Computational Economics* lay open in front of me, a yellow highlighter abandoned next to it. My brain had gone comatose.

"Would you help me with this?" Meg's face had turned bright red from exertion. For the past hour, she'd methodically gone through the living room, moving furniture flush against the walls and stashing away anything breakable. Strands of blond hair had escaped their braid and fell in her eyes as she inched the heavy sofa from its resting place. I'd always envied her hair, but my uber-short cut was easier, even if my own mother said I looked like an orphaned waif.

I helped Meg move the sofa and turned to examine the wide, empty patch of cheap carpet. "What's next?"

"Just sit back and watch." Her eyes sparkled as she drew a large circle on the carpet with chalk, then gathered candles, placed them around the circle, and lit them.

She glanced at an open book on the kitchen counter before

positioning more items around the circle—a steak knife, a paperback book about pirates, a plastic ship, and a rubber alligator from a strand of Mardi Gras beads.

"Where did you get this?" I flipped the book to read its title: *Simple Summonry for Sixth-Sensers*. Its cover had once been leather but now was more like straggling wisps of tanned fibers.

"Estate sale. Some old creepy mansion down on Esplanade."

I shook my head. "Meg, what makes you think this will work?" She'd bitch about it for a month when it didn't, especially after raising her party guests' expectations so high.

She grinned. "What makes you think it *won't* work?"

Throwing my hands up in surrender, I grabbed my textbook and headed for the bedroom. "Call me when the pirate shows up."

I was already deep into the snore-inducing world of macroeconomic modeling when I heard the bedroom door open. Bookmarking my spot, I closed the text and pushed my desk chair back. "Finally giving up? Need me to help move the furniture ?"

The harsh whisper didn't even sound like Meg. "Rhyn, you better come out here."

I turned to look at her. Her face was an eggshell-white oval punctuated with wide blue eyes. Frightened eyes.

My heart rate sped up. "What's wrong?"

Her mouth opened and closed like a fish that had found

itself inexplicably lying in the bottom of a boat with a hook in its mouth. She pointed toward the living room with a shaky index finger.

"What? If this is a joke, I'm going to hurt you." Pushing past her, I walked down the short hallway to the living room.

And froze.

A man stood in the circle she had drawn. A tall, handsome man with dark, wavy hair that reached his broad shoulders, and blue eyes the color of deep cobalt. A scar on his jaw. Hands propped on his hips. A glare on his face.

Pointing at us, he shouted something in French, his voice a strong baritone. Then he glared some more.

I turned back to Meg with raised eyebrows, the question unnecessary.

"I think it's him," she whispered. "Jean Lafitte."

"You foolish trollops. It is my wish for you to break this circle immediately."

We turned back to stare at him as his voice lowered from English back into a soft flurry of French. He mumbled to himself, feeling his way around an invisible cylinder that seemed to have him trapped inside the circle.

He looked like a big, pissed-off mime. One who might be dangerous.

"I don't know how to get rid of him," Meg whispered.

I turned on her, my voice rising into an undignified squeak. "What do you mean you don't know how to get rid of him? What does the book say?"

I grabbed it off the counter and flipped frantically, only to find the last missing. The pages had been ripped out, bits of ragged paper hanging from the binding.

"Why didn't you make sure you had the whole book before you did this?" My question came out in a hiss.

A few tears escaped and trailed down Meg's cheeks. She had folded in on herself, her arms clutching her middle. "I didn't *really* think it would work, not deep down. I just thought it would be funny to try and—"

"What are your names? Answer me, *tout de suite.*"

We whirled at the masculine voice, which sounded as if its owner were accustomed to giving orders. Jean Lafitte—if that's really who it was—stood in the circle with his arms crossed, stance wide. An enormous pistol with a curved handle had been tucked into his belt, which cinched his loose white tunic at his hips. Knee-high boots and black pants completed the pirate ensemble.

Meg walked toward him, gulping in deep breaths. Damn right. It was her mess. Let her deal with it. "I'm Meg, and"— she thumbed over her shoulder at me—"this is Rhyn. Are you really him? Jean Lafitte?"

He cocked his head, a smile quirking up one corner of his mouth. "*Oui,* Mademoiselle Meg." He held his hand out as if to shake hers.

"Meg—no!" I screeched, watching in horror as she stuck out her hand and broke the cylinder. When had Meg turned stupid? Every ridiculous witch movie she'd ever made me watch was clear on the whole no-breaking-a-summoning-circle thing.

Lafitte took her hand and lifted it to his lips, brushing the back of her knuckles with a kiss, then swept past her with long strides, exploring the apartment, opening doors, pulling out drawers, and glancing behind furniture.

He stopped suddenly and turned back to us, rooted in place as if we'd been stuck to the carpet with Super Glue, mouths agape. "What hour is it?"

Meg looked blank, so I glanced at my watch. "It's after two. In the morning."

"Might I procure transportation? I can offer something in exchange." He reached in a pouch attached to his belt and shook it. The thing sounded as if it were full of coins. "I wish to exchange a small bit of gold for passage to a location outside the city. We have little time."

I'd never seen Meg so shaken. She seemed incapable of speech while I, the sensible half of this friendship, had plenty to say.

"Why do you need transportation?" I asked. "The only place you need to go is back where you came from." Speaking of which. "Where *did* you come from?"

I should have kept my mouth shut. Lafitte's blue gaze latched onto me. "Pardon, mademoiselle... You are a woman, yes? With the hair so short I am unsure..." His gaze raked over my cropped T-shirt and khaki shorts, paused at my legs, rose to study the tiny silver ring in my exposed belly button, and came to rest on my breasts.

I had an annoying urge to comb my hair and explain that I normally dressed better, even though that wasn't true. I was mortified.

"Most fascinating," he said. "We shall discuss this further, if time is sufficient after my business is completed. First, you must provide me with modern currency, if not transportation."

"Does this apartment look like a bank?" I snapped, thinking macroeconomic theory was starting to sound fascinating. It might kill me with boredom but it wouldn't stab me with a piratical cutlass.

Lafitte walked toward me slowly, predatory, and I swallowed the golfball-sized lump of fear in my throat.

I closed my eyes as he neared, the power oozing from him and brushing across my skin. Behind me, a door rattled, then clicked shut.

By the time I'd turned around, he was gone. What an idiot. It hadn't been power wafting across my skin; it was the air he'd stirred up breezing past me.

"Oh, thank God. He's gone." Meg sat on the floor with a thud.

I stared at her. "What do you mean, thank God he's gone?" My voice cracked. "We just loosened the freakin' pirate Jean Lafitte on the French Quarter on a Friday night! He'll rob somebody, or kill somebody, or, or, or *pillage*. You have to go after him."

"Are you nuts?" Meg rubbed her eyes. "I'm going to throw that stupid book away and go to bed. Wait." She sat up. "Do you realize what this means? We can summon anybody! Maybe we could get Marie Laveau for Halloween—do a whole voodoo priestess theme."

My anger rose sharp and hot. I shoved the book from the counter into the trashcan, grabbed my purse, and stalked toward the door.

"Where are you going?" Meg got to her feet.

"I'm going to find Jean Lafitte before he kills somebody and it's our fault," I shouted. "Make that *your* fault."

I let the door slam behind me and took the steps two at a time.

Three

I STOOD AT THE open courtyard gate and sent frantic looks up and down Royal Street. Where would I go if I were a 200-year-old pirate suddenly loosed upon the modern world, intent on rape and murder? Well, that answer was obvious.

I headed for Bourbon Street.

Hurrying along the sidewalks of lower Bourbon, I rushed toward the touristy part that stretched between St. Louis Cathedral and Canal Street. The perfect spot for a pirate to commit any number of horrible crimes.

It might be mid-September, but New Orleans clung to summer as if it feared losing its reputation as an outpost of hell, at least in terms of weather. Sweat ran down my back. I broke into a run until I reached the touristed areas. The bars and restaurants sent savory aromas and brash trills of sound into the thick night air, and throngs of the drunk and the brave wandered down the middle of the street. I hadn't gone half a block before I spotted him a couple of blocks ahead, staring in a store window and laughing.

He moved on and I followed, trying to dodge a clump of

tourists moving *en masse* down the sidewalk. By the time I untangled myself, I'd lost him again. Slowing, I glanced in the shop window he'd been studying with such amusement a few moments earlier (sex toys, OMG), then continued a slow walk, checking out open storefronts along the way, hoping to glimpse him again.

I'd reached the 500 block of Royal when I was jerked sideways into an alley between two buildings and found myself pinned to the aging brick wall by a big, frowning pirate.

"You would make a poor spy, mademoiselle," he said, and from my up-close vantage point, his size and strength felt overwhelming. He smelled of tobacco and cinnamon, and he was six-two or more, broad-shouldered and hard-muscled.

I tried to slow my heart down so I wouldn't sound like what I was—a breathless, scared MBA student. "I just wanted to make sure you didn't hurt anybody."

He was essentially a ghost, right? Why did he feel so damned solid and warm?

"And why would I hurt anyone, little... Repeat your name, *s'il vous plaît*?"

"Rhyn," I whispered. "Kathryn."

He stepped back, and I took a deep, ragged breath. As much as I wanted to run home and hide, I couldn't in good conscience leave the corporeal ghost of Jean Lafitte wandering around on his own. I needed to find out what he wanted, get it for him, and pray he'd leave peaceably.

"Kathryn, why did your cowardly friend summon me?" he

asked. "To what end did she intend to use me?"

God, how stupid was this going to sound? "She, uh, wanted to take you to her *Talk Like a Pirate Day* party." I paused, then added, "I think she expected someone...smaller."

He shook his head and muttered, *"Les jeunes femmes insensées."*

I spoke a little French and had been called worse than a foolish young woman, so I let it slide. At least he wasn't pissed off anymore, just disgusted.

"Where do you want to go?" I asked.
"Do you know the home of Jean-Noël Destréhan? I must reach it before the wizard arrives to send me back to my home."

I couldn't process *wizard*, so I focused on *Destrehan*. "There's a town called Destrehan," I said, thinking. "And there's the Destrehan Plantation." In fact, if I lived through this, I'd be going to the annual fall festival there in a few weeks, eating crawfish bread and remembering this as a very bad dream.

Lafitte's eyes crinkled when he smiled. "The home of my old friend Jean-Noël. *Oui*, that is exactly where I wish to go. You will take me there now."

He clamped a big, strong hand around my wrist and pulled me out of the alley, taking long strides down Bourbon in the direction from which we'd come. I had to trot to avoid being dragged down the street on my chin.

An NOPD officer stood on an adjacent corner, and I

considered screaming for help. But what would I tell him? That I was being dragged through the French Quarter by Jean Lafitte, who wanted transportation to the Destrehan Plantation? We'd both spend the night in lockup. Besides, Lafitte didn't seem interested in raping or pillaging me— probably because I looked poor and he wasn't entirely convinced I was a girl.

"Wait!" I planted my feet and tugged him to a stop. "I don't have a car. I can't take you to Destrehan. Plus it's the middle of the night and the place will be closed. If we took a taxi it would look suspicious."

"I do not need to go inside the house, only to the grounds." We were only a couple of blocks from the river, and the sound of a ship's horn echoed through the Quarter. Jean turned to me with a smile. "Do you possess a vessel? We might sail there."

"Do I *look* like I have a vessel?" Sure, I docked it near Audubon Park, adjacent to the building where I stored my collection of vintage sports cars.

"Bah. Useless woman." Lafitte turned and strode toward Decatur Street and the river, drunken tourists instinctively moving out of his way and more than a few women taking a second, appreciative glance.

Good Lord. He'd steal one of the French Quarter carriages if I didn't get him under control.

"Wait for me!" I ran after him.

He stopped and looked back at me. "My apologies,

mademoiselle, but I do not have time for an assignation"—he swept those intense blue eyes over me again, stopping on my chest—"as enjoyable as that might be since you do not appear to be entirely a boy."

"I don't want to assignate..." I sputtered, heat spreading across my face. "I'll take you to Destrehan if you promise that, afterward, you'll go back to wherever you came from."

He grinned. "*Très bien*, Mademoiselle Kathryn. Lead me to your horse."

Four

I MANEUVERED MEG'S TRUSTY steed, an aging VW Beetle of a mottled, sickly color that had once been yellow, along the winding curves of Jefferson Highway, driving Jean Lafitte to Destrehan Plantation. He sat in the passenger seat, long legs almost bumping his chin as we rattled along. Meg, not surprisingly, had refused to come with us.

Lafitte wasn't complaining about the cramped quarters but, rather, watched the passing scenery and my operation of the manual transmission with equal fascination.

And the man—ghost, spirit, whatever—wouldn't shut up.

"Tell me the meaning of these red and green lights that hang over the path. Where is the river in relation to our location? Who is this Burger King—does he rule New Orleans or is America now a monarchy? Are there still fortunes to be made from profiteering?"

I answered the ones I could, although I could tell he wasn't convinced that Burger King had no royal powers. "Explain how profiteering works."

"I procure goods and sell them to local merchants for a

19

lower cost than they are able to obtain them elsewhere," he said. "In turn, they sell the goods to their customers for lower than the merchants who do not purchase them from me."

"Supply and demand, undercutting the competition. It's good business." I nodded. Sound economic theory, and not illegal *per se*. "What kind of goods are you interested in procuring, and how would you get them?" Were there ghost-driven supply chains in his world?

"Tobacco, spices, spirits, even"—he reached over and jerked the T-shirt down to bare my shoulder, peering down the neck and almost making me drive the bug into the side of the Pontchartrain Expressway overpass—"personal items for ladies. As for where my men and I obtain our goods, it is primarily from Spanish vessels, whose crews are evil scoundrels unfit to live even in hell itself and the sworn enemies of France."

Right, I'd forgotten for a moment. French pirate. Evil Spaniards. Thank God I came from good Irish stock.

A Jefferson Parish Sheriff's Office cruiser slowed as it passed us and I held my breath, praying we wouldn't be stopped. Beside me, Lafitte pulled that bigass pistol from beneath his tunic, where he'd at least had the good sense to tuck it before parading along Bourbon Street.

We stopped at a red light and he eyed the deputy in the adjacent car, who eyed him back. "Should I kill him?" Lafitte asked, much as one might ask for the salt and pepper at the dinner table.

Oh. My. God. In. Heaven.

"No!" My voice squeaked. "Don't even *look* at him. Put that thing away and don't shoot anyone or I won't take you anywhere." Jeez-Louise.

He raised an eyebrow as if to say what we both knew—that if he chose to shoot anyone, including me, I couldn't do a damned thing to stop him.

"Please?"

"Bah. *Très bien.*" He tucked the pistol away and pulled a long knife from his boot instead.

If I lived through this, Meg was so dead.

Five

I PARKED THE BEETLE a few hundred yards down River Road from the plantation house and followed Jean Lafitte on foot as he strode across the moonlight-dappled grounds, keeping himself hidden behind the trees. Guess he had plenty of experience at skulking. Me, not so much. I tripped every other step.

He paused next to the small building that housed the gift shop, drawn by something in the window. I huffed up next to him and followed his gaze to a small painting of himself, according to the plaque beneath it. The artist had missed the mark, badly. The painted Jean Lafitte had a nose hooked like a boomerang, small beady black eyes, a bad do-rag covering his head, and a knife clutched between his blackened teeth.

I waited for him to curse, or shout, or break the window—something to show his dismay at being turned from an extremely handsome man into an ugly caricature. Instead, he chuckled and moved back into the shadows. "It is good to be remembered, is it not?"

"Oh, you're remembered," I said. "I grew up in Jean Lafitte,

Louisiana. It's a small town south of here, near Barataria."

He stopped and turned so quickly I ran into him. "You will take me there in your wheeled horse next, *oui*?"

That was so not happening.

But what *was* I going to do with him? He claimed Meg had summoned him from "the Beyond," whatever that meant. Heaven? Hell? The planet Zoltan?

We were well behind the plantation house now, and my eyes had adjusted to the surroundings, illuminated by the moonlight filtering through the sweeping branches of massive live oaks. The sky felt bigger out here. I'd forgotten how many stars there were once you left the city lights behind.

Lafitte had stopped a few yards ahead of me to examine the trees. He ran his hands along the bark of one, then another—circling them, reading their textures with his fingers as if scanning a text in braille.

"What are you looking for?" I whispered, creeped out by the hooting of an owl, the rustle of the wind, the ghostly wail of a ship's horn wafting down the river—even as I realized those things shouldn't scare me nearly as much as the fact that I'd driven a dead pirate across three Louisiana parishes in the middle of the night.

He ignored me, placing his back at the last tree he'd found and pacing away from it.

After twenty steps, he stopped, knelt, and used his knife to start digging into the soil.

"You have buried treasure here?" I envisioned a trunk full

of gold and gems, antique coins that would be worth a fortune today. The pirate Lafitte was rumored to have stashed gold all over South Louisiana, but no one had ever found any. Not for lack of trying; people had been digging up half the state for the past two centuries.

"Only a small bit here and more in other areas," he said. "In my day, one never knew when one might need some.... Bah, I do not know the phrase."

"Getaway money?" I ventured.

He laughed. "*Oui*, money in order to get away, as you say. But even in the Beyond, one can make use of gold."

I dropped to my knees facing him, pulled a penknife from my purse, and helped him dig. We worked in silence until, finally, I struck a solid object. "I have something."

Moving out of his way, I let him ply his knife to my side of the excavation, and he grinned. "*Voila!*" He pulled a small glass container from the earth and gently wiped the wet soil away from it. Pulling off its stopper-like lid, he reached inside and took out one of many coins—it was filled with them. He rubbed the coin on his thigh, back and forth, and then held it out to me. Even in the moonlight, it picked up a gleam.

"Gold, Kathryn. It is still valued in your time, yes?"

"Oh, yes," I said, transfixed. My hand trembled as I took the coin from him and ran my fingers across its surface. It was too dark to tell what was printed on it, but it was old and it was gold.

A branch snapped somewhere behind us, which I thought

nothing of until the pirate grabbed my arm and jerked me to my feet. I stuck the coin in my pocket.

"We must take shelter," he whispered. "It is that damnable, meddlesome wizard."

Wizard? I'd hoped that whole wizard thing had been a joke. Next came the question: whose side was I on? Would the wizard help me escape the pirate, or would the wizard be worse?

I didn't have time to ponder my answer; Lafitte decided for me.

"*Dépêchez-vous*, Kathryn. Run!" Clutching the jar of gold coins in one hand and dragging me along with the other, Lafitte sprinted toward the back of the plantation house, which rose dark and solid beneath the moonlight.

A rose bush exploded into a hurricane of leaves and blooms to our right as Lafitte dragged me up the back stairs and ducked to the right, away from the door.

We crouched at the corner of the wide verandah. "What happened?" I whispered.

"Arrogant wizard," Lafitte mumbled. "He tries to hurt me with magic and dispatches only leaves and flowers into the air."

A man's voice, decidedly British and unnaturally calm, came to us from somewhere nearby. "Come now, Captain Lafitte. Let's not drag this out longer than necessary, shall we? We both know how this encounter will end."

"Ah, but the fates have not yet been decided, Monsieur St.

Simon." Lafitte's voice rang out as calm and pleasant as that of the other man—the wizard, I assumed. "I have a guest with me this evening who might assure a longer visit than usual."

Lafitte poked me in the side. "Tell him your name, girl," he whispered.

"Uh, Kathryn Williams here." My voice sounded squeaky; he'd think I was a child. "Sir."

"Bloody hell." The wizard didn't sound happy to hear me. "How did you get in the middle of this, Kathryn Williams. Are you human?"

What a stupid question. "Of course I'm hu—"

"Enough," Lafitte hissed, pulling me around the corner. He used his elbow to knock the glass out of a window, then reached through, unlocked it, and tugged it open.

As soon as the window casing left the sill, an alarm sent shrill, deafening whoops of noise echoing into the night. *"Mon Dieu, qu'est-ce que c'est?"* Lafitte grabbed my arm and shouted to be heard over the racket.

"It's a security alarm!" I struggled to escape his grasp. "The police will come soon."

I thought that would make him release me and see to his own safety, but no. The pirate laughed. "What fun the wizard will have with the *gendarmes*. Let us go inside."

He shoved me through the open window ahead of him, and dragged me through the house as if he knew his way around. I guess he remembered it from his human life. We raced up a staircase and into a room off a hallway. The whole house was dimly illuminated by the moonlight.

Sirens sounded in the distance, growing closer. "That's the police," I said. "They'll arrest you, or worse." The way my night was going, they'd shoot at the pirate and kill me instead.

"Bah. The wizard will take care of them, and I have business to do before he sends me back to Old Orleans," Lafitte said. He dragged me across the darkened room, and I heard him fumbling with something. How could he see?

A few seconds later, there was a small burst of flame as the pirate lit a small lantern.

The room around us became visible in the soft light—a small bedroom with jade green walls and gleaming white millwork and fireplace. The bed, not much wider than a modern twin-size, had been covered in a white quilt, and white curtains hung from the full canopy.

"How did you know where to find the lantern?" I had been on tours of the plantation house a few times but not in the middle of the night with what sounded like half of the St. Charles Parish Sheriff's Office en route. I felt a sudden urge to cry and prayed I'd wake up and discover this was a really bad nightmare.

"One must always be prepared, and I came here often during my human life. Sit there and do not move, Kathryn." Lafitte pointed to a straight-backed chair cushioned in red velvet, and I did as I was told. The deputies should be here any moment to rescue me, after all. Their squad cars had turned off the main highway with squealing tires, followed by the sudden absence of the deafening sirens. The flashing blue lights pulsed through the sheer draperies.

Meanwhile, Lafitte opened the jar of gold coins and stuffed them into the pouch attached to his belt. Not all would fit, so he jammed the rest inside his tunic. He left a few—maybe a dozen or so—in the jar and replaced the lid.

I kept waiting to hear multiple pairs of deputy boots pounding up the staircase. Instead, I heard voices outside. Not raised voices, but calm ones, followed by slamming car doors, revving engines, and cars driving away.

I had a sudden moment of clarity. They didn't know I was here. Somehow, the wizard was sending them away exactly as the pirate had anticipated. And I, like an idiot, sat here as if in this ridiculous situation by choice. The wizard was not a threat; he was my way out.

I screamed, not caring if the pirate Lafitte stabbed me. I screamed until my voice was raw. I screamed until I realized the pirate sat calmly in the chair behind the writing desk, watching me with his armed crossed over his bulging shirt of gold coins. The edges of his mouth were upticked in a smile.

"Why didn't you stop me from screaming?" I was oddly offended that my first-ever blood-curdling screams earned nothing more than a smile. He could at least have tried to shut me up.

Lafitte grinned and jerked his head toward the door. "You have saved me the trouble of having to find the wizard, Mademoiselle Kathryn. *Merci* ."

Now I heard them, the footfalls on the steps from the first floor, then the creaking of the hallway floor. The doorknob turned and, finally, the wooden door swung open.

"You are quite the most bothersome pirate I have ever had the displeasure of meeting, Lafitte." The man in the doorway was middle-aged, dressed in a stylish silk shirt and tailored trousers, and of medium height and weight. I doubt I'd have noticed him on the street, not because he was unattractive but because he was so very ordinary. His salt-and-pepper hair, heavy on the salt, was pulled back in a short ponytail and he looked at me through blue-gray eyes that sparked with intelligence.

"And you, I gather, are his screaming hostage? What was your name—Kathryn?"

I nodded. "You're a w-w-wizard?" I had developed a sudden stutter.

"This is our wizard sentinel, Gerald St. Simon," Lafitte said. "It is his job to ensure that lovely young women such as yourself do not learn about the existence of thieves and ruffians such as Jean Lafitte. Is this not correct, monsieur?"

"Quite." The wizard wasn't happy. Then again, other than an exploding rose bush, I had only Lafitte's word that wizards existed. He could be a really well-dressed plumber. "I had to do quite some spellwork to rid myself of the deputies, and now I shall have to call in a Blue Congress cleanup team to erase your presence from the plantation house. You've caused a lot of trouble this time, captain."

"Bah, I have merely provided you with an evening of entertainment."

Neither of them paid any attention to me, which was fine. If the so-called wizard wasn't blocking my path, I'd have slipped out and let them deal with each other. Just in case he was a wizard, I didn't want to be given the rose-bush treatment, however, so I stayed put.

"Well, let's get on with this, shall we?" The wizard moved several pieces of furniture, including a bench that he set across the doorway, further blocking my potential exit. He took a small jar from his pocket and sprinkled a white powder that looked like salt on the floor, drawing first a triangle and then a circle that overlapped one corner of the triangle.

"Captain Lafitte? Let's make the rest of this easy, shall we?"

Lafitte smiled and got to his feet, jingling a little from all the coins in his pouch and shirt but also shaking the jar he held with its dozen coins. "Certainly, Sentinel. I have what I came to find, and will be pleased to return to my own home."

He stepped inside the triangle and didn't argue when the wizard reached out and grabbed the jar of coins. Instead, he winked at me. All the gold he'd kept was our little joke.

"You know I won't allow you to take this with you," the wizard said. "I'll donate it to the upkeep of the Destrehan Plantation, which seems only fair." He handed me the jar. Apparently, he didn't see me as a threat to run away with it.

"*Oui*, my old friend Jean-Noël Destréhan would like the gold to be used thus." Lafitte nodded, then turned to me and bowed slightly—but not too much. I'm sure he didn't want his shirt to jingle with all the gold he was taking with him. "*Bonsoir*, Kathryn. Perhaps we shall meet again."

Oh, God. I hoped not.

I'm not sure what I expected from the wizard. A magic wand, maybe, or some Latin incantations. He simply pricked his finger with the flick of a small knife, let a drop of blood fall on the white powder, pointed his finger at the bloody spot, and said "Old Barataria."

Lafitte was grinning when his image faded and disappeared with a small pop that sounded like a bubble bursting.

"Well, now. What should I do with you, Kathryn?" The wizard—because after the pirate's disappearance I firmly believed he was exactly that, and I had the shaky hands to prove it—turned his blue-gray gaze on me. "First, how did you summon him? For the love of all that is holy, *why* did you summon him?"

"It wasn't me, it was my roommate," I said, climbing to my feet and holding out the jar for him to take, lest he think I was a willing participant in this nightmare. "She kind of thought he'd be like Captain Jack Sparrow."

The wizard closed his eyes and let out an exasperated sigh. "It's all Johnny Depp's fault. Blasted movies. Is that your car outside? The VW?"

I nodded. "He made me bring him here."

"I'm sure he did." The wizard's smile was kind. "And now I shall make you drive me to your home. I need to meet your roommate."

Six

MEG AND I WALKED in silence to Café du Monde for our regular Saturday-morning fix of beignets and coffee. I still wore the clothes I'd had on yesterday, even though I didn't remember going to bed last night.

I did remember dreaming, though. "I'll be glad when Talk Like a Pirate Day is over." I tapped the powdered sugar off the beignet into my coffee. "I freakin' *dreamed* about Jean Lafitte last night."

Meg laughed. "So did I, and then I dreamed some middle-aged British guy brought you home early this morning and did some kind of hocus-pocus on us."

That sounded familiar to me, too, but as soon as I tried to remember it, to put a face on it, the wisp of memory slipped away. I needed caffeine, badly.

"You still going to try and summon Jean Lafitte?" I asked, hoping Meg had changed her mind.

She shook her head and took a loud slurp of coffee. "No, that was a stupid idea. Funny thing, though. I can't find the summoning book. Do you remember seeing it?"

I tried to remember but for the life of me, the whole evening was a blur. Proof that macroeconomics are bad for the brain.

We pushed our chairs back, and Meg wove through the crowds of people already lining up for a chance at one of the small café tables. I stayed behind, digging in my rumpled pockets for tip money. I pulled out a large round coin, its edges slightly irregular. On the front was a man's head, the date 1800, and some words in Spanish.

I pressed hands against my suddenly throbbing temples, trying to pin down flashing images of digging in the soil at night, a strange man, a glass jar. But the memory, idea— whatever it was—disappeared as quickly as it came.

I didn't know where the coin came from, or how I got it, but it was all the change I had. Shrugging, I tossed it on the table as a tip and ran to catch up with Meg.

LAGNIAPPE: THE SENTINELS MULTIVERSE

A brief introduction to the multiverse of the Sentinels of New Orleans, where gods and monsters, wizards and merfolk, loups-garou and corporeal ghosts walk among us in the Crescent City.

The World

THE SENTINELS OF NEW Orleans series is set in New Orleans and Southeast Louisiana after the barriers between the city and the otherworld, the Beyond, were weakened by Hurricane Katrina.

Think of an iceberg (something one should never see in New Orleans unless the faeries are misbehaving). The modern city we all know is the part above the water line. The first few inches of ice below it make up the lawless border town of Old Orleans, where the historical undead still roam and creatures of all species mingle with unpredictable results. Electricity works in a few parts of town, but not in most. The sun never shines, and the moon is always full.

Below the border ice is the vast Beyond, where other species live in their own ancestral realms. Elfheim, Vampyre, and Faerie are the largest outposts, but not the only ones. There are said to be parts of the Beyond deep, deep below the surface of space and time, where no one has ever ventured— and lived to tell about it.

Some species have coexisted, undetected, among humans

for generations. Wizards, the largest group other than perhaps the fae and the most powerful in the human world, have lived among us since the beginnings of time. Likewise, many of the were-creatures and shapeshifters, including werewolves and merfolk, have long mainstreamed in our world.

Meet the major species.

The Wizards

T HE WIZARDS WIELD DIFFERENT forms of magic, and are the largest species other than perhaps the fae (who are so busy changing appearance they haven't had time to conduct a census). Wizards have always lived in the human world, where their magic is most effective, although they keep their presence a secret to humans. The wizards have fielded many wars over the centuries, most recently a civil war in 1976 when a group of rogue wizards tried to overthrow their ruling council, the Congress of Elders. The Elders prevailed. One of the initial rogue supporters who ultimately remained loyal to the Elders was Gerald St. Simon, who as punishment was sent to the outpost of New Orleans as sentinel. Sentinels have traditionally been the border guards/gatekeepers between the human world and the Beyond.

A wizard is not allowed to practice magic outside his or her own home without holding a license from the Congress of Elders. Licensed wizards are divided by his or her dominant magic in one of the four congresses.

Red Congress wizards are dominant in physical magic;

some use wands or a ring to channel their magic, but it isn't necessary. They are the second-smallest congress, and many work for the Elders in some capacity. Most sentinels are Red Congress wizards, but not all. Gerald St. Simon, mentor to series protagonist DJ Jaco, is a Red Congress wizard and was the sentinel of the New Orleans region prior to Hurricane Katrina.

Green Congress wizards are dominant in ritual magic and potions; they are the largest congress. DJ Jaco, the lead character in the series, is a Green Congress wizard and currently the sentinel of the New Orleans/Gulf South region. Most Green Congress wizards work in engineering, science, or academics. DJ holds a degree in chemistry from Tulane University in New Orleans, although her mentor, Gerald St. Simon, tutored her privately in magic and basic human studies.

Blue Congress wizards specialize in illusion and creation. They tend to be artists, writers, musicians, or academics specializing in humanities and liberal arts fields.

Yellow Congress wizards specialize in mental magic— psychic abilities, for example. They are the smallest congress. Most work in healthcare, social work, or psychiatry, or in the entertainment industry. Many are popular on talk-show circuits.

The Elves

THE ELVES ARE FEWER in number than the wizards and fae, but are arguably more powerful, especially outside the human world where the wizards' physical magic doesn't work reliably, if at all.

The elves' ancestral home in the Beyond is Elfheim, largest in geographic size. Elfheim is the only region of the Beyond, other than Faerie, that is not always dark and under a full moon.

Elven magic is primarily mental. They are adept at mind-reading and, if touching their victim, can retrieve memories and manipulate thoughts and emotions. They possess the arts of scrying and empathy, as well as some elemental skills associated with each of the four clans: the most powerful of the Tân, for example, the Fire Elves, can cause items (or people) within their proximity to burst into flames. Earth, air, and water elves can do telekinesis within their respective elements.

The elves are ruled by a Synod of the four clan chiefs. As the series begins, the head of the Elven Synod is Mace Banyan, chief of the Aer Clan.

Over the years, as the elves became disgusted with the advent of technology in the human world and retreated into Elfheim, the four ancient staffs of power belonging to the clans were lost. One, Mahout, the staff of the Tân, was found by wizard DJ Jaco in New Orleans after Hurricane Katrina and, recognizing her as possessing the skills of its clan, claimed her as its owner. She has since renamed it Charlie.

The Fae

THE PEOPLE OF FAERIE make up the largest population of preternaturals in the Beyond, and their ancestral lands are second-largest outside the human world (behind sparsely populated Elfheim). The fae have a rigid class system and two elemental types of powers: science and illusion. Faerie is a monarchy ruled by Sabine, who is old and childless.

Sabine has two nephews who are eligible to succeed her on the throne: Florian, the Prince of Summer, and his younger brother Christof, the Prince of Winter. Both Florian and Christof can wield both the magic of The Arch (science) and The Academy (illusion), which is a requirement of the monarch.

The lesser houses of Autumn and Spring do not have rulers capable of wielding both powers.

Due to centuries of political infighting, the fae have made few attempts to live among humans, and it is illegal for non-royals to cross the veil without permission. The feared Fae Hunters, based in New Orleans, are the one exception—it is their job to track down those who have crossed the veil illegally and return them to Faerie. The Captain of the Fae Hunters is Faulkner Hearne, eldest son of the Prince of Autumn, who passed the throne to his younger brother in order to lead the Hunters.

There is a large population of non-royal faeries, all of whom wield one or the other type of power to some small degree. At the bottom of the social ladder are those fae with a noticeable amount of human blood and the hybrids, who are the products of experimentation by holders of Arch or Academy magic to cross-breed potential monarchs. It usually ends badly.

Faeries cannot handle metals without injury or death, so fae-human hybrids often do metalwork or devise tools that do not require metals. The fae are fascinated with human popular culture.

Shapeshifters and Weres

WERE-CREATURES ARE FORMER humans who have been infected with various strains of lycanthropy and whose shifts are controlled by the phases of the moon. Their shifts are painful and require recovery time. Werewolves are the most common types of weres. All weres belong to a pack structure of some sort.

Shapeshifters are born, not made, and they are able to mainstream as humans but shift at will using magic. Some shapeshifters are outliers, such as Alexander Warin, a canine shifter who does not belong to a family of shifters. Other shifters make up defined species, such as merfolk and other water species, including nixes and nymphs.

A third type of were is unique to South Louisiana, the loup-garou. The loup-garou is a former human who carries a magically cursed strain of lycanthropy. Loups-garou are large rogue werewolves of a particularly vicious nature that do not adhere to pack structure. They are rarely able to assimilate safely into human society, with little control over their shifts, and are usually killed if they are not willing to live in the

Beyond.

In the human world, many weres and some shifters, because of their extraordinary physical strength and ability to heal almost anything (weres, but not shifters, are sensitive to silver), work in security, military, and law enforcement positions.

Those deemed particularly skilled at weapons usage and investigation are trained by the wizarding Elders as enforcers—the elite killers of the preternatural world. In the Sentinels series, Alexander Warin is an enforcer.

Vampires

V AMPIRES LIVE BOTH IN the human world and in the Beyond, in their ancestral land of the Realm of Vampyre. While vampires gain their nutrition by feeding from other vampires of the opposite sex, the blood of humans is sweet and addictive to them.

The vampires who live in the human world are strictly ruled by Regents, who all report to the Vice-Regent, Garrett Melnick. The Regent of the New Orleans area is Etienne Boulard, who owns a club called L'Amour Sauvage in the French Quarter.

The vampires have very strict rules against revealing their true nature to humans; they can feed only from willing humans, and then must perform memory modifications. Creating a new vampire, which involves killing and draining the human, is strictly prohibited without express permission of the Vice-Regent.

Although strictly self-governed, the vampires have over the

centuries proven untrustworthy political allies for other species. They will support the group that best serves their own interests.

Minor Preternaturals

A NUMBER OF SPECIES, smaller in number, also can be found in the Beyond, ranging from goblins (who like to drink alcohol to excess), dwarves (who like to fight to excess) and Greek gods (who like to spar among themselves to excess). None of these groups has more than minimal power in the human world, and many live in the border town of Old Orleans, lacking ancestral lands of their own.

The Historical Undead

THE HISTORICAL UNDEAD ARE formerly famous humans given immortality by the magic of human memory. As long as they are remembered and spoken of by humans, they can exist in corporeal form in the Beyond and even in the human world, at least for a while. The more they are remembered, the longer they can stay without retreating to Old Orleans to recharge their immortal batteries. They generally live in the border town nearest the place where they lived their human lives.

As arguably the most famous New Orleanian (with towns, wildlife habitats, schools, streets, and businesses named after him), the early 19th-century French pirate Jean Lafitte is the strongest of the historical undead and is able to remain in modern New Orleans as long as he wishes. He maintains his home in the Old Orleans outpost of Old Barataria, which mirrors the place he lived during his human life, but he also rents out the posh Eudora Welty Suite located in the Hotel

Monteleone on Royal Street in modern New Orleans under the name John Lafayette. He pays a year at a time and comes and goes as he wishes.

Other famous New Orleanians who have appeared thus far in the Sentinels of New Orleans series include voodoo priestess Marie Laveau, jazz great Louis Armstrong, authors William Faulkner and Truman Capote, and former governor Huey P. Long.

ALEX, THE PIG

"Alex, the Pig" was inspired by the book blog Pearls Cast Before a McPig and its namesake, Sullivan McPig. The original story appeared as flash fiction on that website in 2013. It features wizard sentinel Drusilla "DJ" Jaco, the narrator of the Sentinels of New Orleans novels; her significant something-or-other Alexander Warin, a canine shapeshifter; and her friend Rene Delachaise, a merman. Alex, aka Mr. Straight and Narrow, tends to get discombobulated when confronted with messy things like family gatherings...and, apparently, cursed leprechauns.

For those interested in timelines, "Alex, the Pig" takes place between the events of River Road *and* Elysian Fields.

I'M NOT THE WORLD'S most perceptive wizard, but even I could tell Alex Warin was hiding something.

My former partner and current significant something-or-other stood outside my front door, which was about thirty feet from his front door. Yeah, we were neighbors, which complicated things in so many ways.

He tapped the edge of the threshold with the toe of his boot, studied the door facing, and picked at a peeling spot of paint. He did everything, in other words, except look me in the eye. He'd begun the conversation with the weather and finally admitted he wanted to ask a favor.

"Okay, fine. What's this favor you want me to do?" It must be something bad. Last time I'd seen this expression, he'd been working up the nerve to ask me to pose as his longtime girlfriend at a dinner with his mother. He still owed me for that debacle.

"It's no big deal, really." Alex followed me into the front parlor of my house and perched on the edge of an armchair. He appeared ready to make a quick escape, which ratcheted up my suspicion another level.

"So, what is this no-big-deal favor?" I crossed my arms and

waited, not wanting to give him the wrong impression by sitting down. This was gonna be something I'd hate.

"I have an enforcer run." He sat back in the chair and ran his hands through his dark, always shaggy hair, which made me want to do the same thing. I loved his hair. Another reason to remain standing and avoid getting distracted by something like sex. "I've gotta apprehend this young wizard out in Grammercy and take her to a hearing. Elders are deciding whether or not to strip her powers. She was on track to test for Blue Congress in the next year or two."

"Good grief, what'd she do?" Blue Congress wizards had cool skills in illusion and creation. "And what does it have to do with me?"

"She cursed a leprechaun for making a pass at her; they're a protected species, you know. I need you to, uh, pet-sit for a couple of hours while I'm gone."

I processed this, trying to fill in what he wasn't telling me. A lot. For one thing, Alex didn't have a pet.

"If you won't tell me the truth, find some other sucker to help." I shrugged and walked into the kitchen. I'm really not that bitchy; I just know what works.

Less than a minute passed until he followed me, but not before I heard the front door open and then close again. I had been pulling out leftover Chinese and dumping it into a bowl to microwave for dinner, but turned when my cat Sebastian, a cranky chocolate Siamese, turned into a Halloween cliché, arching his back, baring his pointy teeth, and bulging his crossed blue eyes.

Alex stood in the kitchen doorway. He wore a black muscle shirt, black running pants, black boots, and held a black leash. With a pig on the end. The pig was more of a medium-charcoal color.

Intelligent words escaped me. "It's a pig."

"Well, it's actually a cursed leprechaun. He's, uh, not cooperating, so we need to keep an eye on him until he changes back. His name's Seamus."

"Sure it is." I exchanged uneasy glances with the porcine leprechaun. This was no cute little teacup pig. He was charcoal with a tuft of red hair that sprung at a ninety-degree angle off the top of his head, positioned between his floppy pig ears. He could feed a family of ten for a week, from bacon breakfasts to pork steak dinners. "What do you mean he isn't cooperating?"

As if on cue, Seamus lowered his head, fixed me with a piggy glare, and turned. His hooves clattered across my living room floor. I ran to stop him before he reached my sofa. "No pigs on the couch!"

Seamus had no aspirations to sofa-jump. Instead, he methodically pulled each upholstered seat cushion onto the floor, rooted them around with his snout, and flopped onto his side right in the middle of my custom fleur de lis upholstery, releasing a big, hoglike sigh.

"That pig can't stay here," I hissed, turning to face my empty kitchen. My door stood ajar. Out the window,

I saw Alex's SUV turn the corner from my house and race down Magazine Street toward downtown.

He was going to pay for this.

I sat in the armchair for a while, listening to Seamus snore and wondering where I could take my sofa cushions to be de-swined. This problem called for chocolate.

Who knew pig-cursed leprechauns liked Snickers bars? Seamus rolled to his trotters mid-snore, snout twitching like a radio receiver as he hoofed it toward me.

"Gimme."

Oh. My. God. The pig could talk.

"No. Go back and lie down."

He nipped at my knee, tearing my jeans and breaking skin. I'd need a freaking rabies shot. "Gimme choclit."

I tossed the candy bar in the floor, watching in horror as he ate it, wrapper and all. "Uh. What else do you need?" I could be nice. Leprechauns had terrible reputations for unpleasantness. The joke in the prete community was that their pending extinction could be blamed on the fact that they didn't even like each other enough to breed.

Rumor had it that they could grant wishes, though, if one were willing to pay the price.

"Taters."

"I have frozen French fries. You want those?" They had freezer burn and were at least a year old, but he was a pig. He couldn't be that damned picky.

"Ketchup."

"Okey-dokey then." I went into the kitchen, beat off the worst of the ice crystals from the fries, and spread them on a cookie sheet. While they heated, I rifled through the assortment of outdated condiments in the fridge and finally unearthed a bottle of ketchup with about a half inch left in the bottom. It had only expired a couple of months ago.

Into the ketchup bottle went an inch of water. A good shake to mix it up, and it was ready to pour over the fries when I pulled them from the oven.

So preoccupied was I with my culinary preparations that when someone knocked on my back door, I just reached over and opened it without checking to see who it was. Only then did I realize I could be letting anybody in, like my annoying neighbor Quince Randolph, of whose species I was still suspicious.

But it was my merman buddy Rene Delachaise, who held up a white bag that smelled enticingly like hot beignets.

"Quick, hide those." I snatched the bag from him and lobbed it to the top of the fridge. I loved beignets, and I didn't want to share them with a talking Irish pig.

"Why did you..." He trailed off, his dark eyes widening at something behind me.

I didn't even need to turn around. "It's a pig. I'm making him some French fries."

Seamus added in his grunting pigspeak: "Wid ketchup."

"Yep. Wid ketchup." I pulled the cookie sheet from the oven, slid the fries onto a plate, and coated them with my watered-down ketchup. I set it in the floor and stood next to Rene.

"His table manners need some work, babe," Rene muttered.

Seamus rooted the red-coated fries onto the floor and ate them from what had been my recently shiny and polished hardwood. Alex would be cleaning the floor along with my upholstery.

Seamus raised his head and sniffed the air. "Beer."

"Will you grant me a wish if I get you a beer?" I could have him get rid of Quince Randolph. Or undo Jake Warin's loup-garou curse. Maybe give the wizards' flunky Adrian Hoffman a bad case of the boils.

"No. Ain't give wish." Seamus clattered to the corner of the kitchen and snorted at us as he took a whiz on my floor.

All right. That did it. He could lounge on my sofa cushions. Eat my past-date food. But he could not relieve himself on my hardwood.

"I'll get you a beer." I opened the fridge door and whispered to Rene. "See if that black leash is still in the living room."

"Move, pig." He edged past Seamus, careful not to touch him.

I ignored the six-pack of Abita Amber and slammed the fridge door. "Oops, I'm all out. Let's go next door. Alex always has Turbo Dog."

"Beer?" Seamus peered at me through little piggy eyes. I'd never be able to watch the movie *Babe* again.

"Really good beer. The best," I assured him, retrieving the

key ring I kept hanging at the edge of my counter and removing the key to Alex's house. "You'll like Turbo Dog. It's the most stout-like of our local beers."

I had no idea if that were true, only that I wanted to keep Seamus focused on me while Rene sneaked up behind him with the leash.

He looped the leash over the pig's head, but didn't have his feet under him. So when Seamus raced past him at a fast trot, he pulled Rene off-balance and dragged him across half the living room before the merman regained control.

"It ain't gonna be like that, pig!" Rene shouted, using the sofa frame as leverage and pulling the leash taut. "You're going..." He turned to me. "Where's he going?"

"He's going to spend the evening at Alex's house." I held up the key.

Rene was shapeshifter strong, so when Seamus dug in his trotters and refused to walk on the leash, Rene wrapped the leash around his snout so he couldn't bite and picked him up in a tight fireman's carry. "Man, this pig is a load and a half. Must weigh three hundred pounds. Let's go."

We walked next door to Alex's house, ignoring the stares and commentary from the outdoor diners at the pizza place across the street. This was New Orleans; a guy carrying a big black pig over his shoulder wasn't likely the strangest thing they'd ever seen.

I unlocked Alex's front door, Rene shoved Seamus inside, and I pulled the door shut and locked it back.

"He's gonna tear up Alex's house, babe."

"Damn straight. Let's have a beignet." Then I remembered the cleanup job awaiting me in my own kitchen. "On second thought, let's have a pizza. I'm craving sausage."

CAT MON DIEU

"Cat Mon Dieu" is one of a very few stories that feature pirate Jean Lafitte flying solo as he leaves DJ behind to explore the Rouses Supermarket in uptown New Orleans. The short-short originally appeared on the Happy Tails and Tales website in August 2013. Timeline-wise, "Cat Mon Dieu" falls between River Road *and* Elysian Fields.

"STAY IN THE CAR, Jean. Don't move. I have to pick up cat food real quick and... Seriously. Don't move."

"Certainly, *Jolie*." Jean Lafitte smiled at his companion for the evening, the New Orleans wizardess Drusilla Jaco, who had offered to ferry him in her automobile back to his hotel on Royal Street. A meeting with the wizarding Elders concerning his new role as a mapper and guide in the Beyond had just concluded. It would be a most profitable venture.

After all, his was a species given immortality by the magic of human memory, and who was more memorable than the famous privateer Jean Lafitte?

Jean watched as Drusilla strode in a most unladylike manner toward a large warehouse with glass across the front, through which he could see many lights and people. A large sign proclaimed the warehouse *Rouses*.

Drusilla had called the establishment a grocery store, where people in the modern world purchased food. In his human life, Jean had always enjoyed visiting the marketplace. People then had never purchased cats as food, however, and it was hard to imagine this cat food as a delicacy. Perhaps

Drusilla was procuring it for the arrogant shapeshifting hound Alexander Warin, which she insisted on keeping as a pet.

Still, perhaps Jean could use cat food to his advantage. He pulled out the leather pouch he kept tucked beneath his wide belt, and shook its contents into his hand. He had four modern dollars and a half-dozen gold coins he had not yet "laundered," as his merman business partner Rene called it. Jean had no idea what the price of a fine cat filet might be, but surely this would be sufficient.

After stowing his pistol, cutlass, and all but a single knife beneath the seat of the automobile that Drusilla called an *es-you-vee*, Jean approached the glaring lights of the Rouses.

Mon Dieu, such a wide assortment of goods! He wandered up and down long rows of fresh and tinned items, making mental notes of what was available. There were many things here he could resell for great profit in Old Orleans, where fresh foodstuffs were expensive.

A glassed-in display of meat and fish stretched across the back of one row, and Jean paused to look at the array. Such bounty! Signs advertised catfish, shrimp, scallops, beef, chickens...

"Can I help you?" A young man wearing a brown apron with a sign pinned to the strap reading MAX stopped across the counter from Jean.

Perhaps he could curry favor with Drusilla by making a peace offering to the officious shapeshifting dog. "Oui,

Monsieur Max, might you perhaps supply me with three pounds of your finest cat?"

The man blinked. "Beg pardon?"

"Cat," Jean said, enunciating more clearly. "Feline. Perhaps the flank would be the best portion." At the man's wide-eyed expression, he added, "It is for a large dog." A large dog with a large opinion of himself.

"You're joking, right?" Max grinned. "Good one."

Jean narrowed his eyes, and Max's grin faltered. *Mon Dieu*, but he would never understand modern folk. Drusilla had spoken of cat food as if it were a common thing.

"It is my understanding that you sell cat, and I wish to purchase some, monsieur. A young woman was here shortly before myself, also purchasing cat. I ask for no handouts, only to be treated as others are treated." Jean rested a hand on the dagger's hilt, which peeked from beneath his tunic.

"Uh, sure. Certainly sir, I will cut that for you now. Sorry 'bout the misunderstanding." Max took a series of awkward sidesteps and picked up the handle of a telephone much like the one in Jean's hotel suite. "This is Max, back at the meat counter. I need some help pronto for a gentleman who's insisting on a particular cut of cat."

Could one adult man not butcher a feline singlehandedly? Jean shook his head.

Wincing, Max held the phone away from his ear a moment, then repeated in a loud whisper, "Yes, cat. C-A-T. And get here fast. Dude's got a blade."

Ending the call, Max busied himself by jerking a large sheet of white paper from a roll and polishing the scales on which he weighed the meat. He looked up and nodded at someone behind Jean, the same ridiculous grin on his face.

Jean turned and his mood blackened at the sight of a black-uniformed man striding toward them, a pistol strapped to his hip. *Mon Dieu*, a *gendarme*.

"What seems to be the problem here?" The rather corpulent officer tugged on his belt, no doubt to ensure that Jean saw not only the pistol but also the thick club attached to the belt.

"I simply wished to buy some cat." Jean raised his voice. Perhaps if he spoke in a more commanding tone, he could make himself understood. "Cat food. For a dog."

The officer's shoulders relaxed and he frowned at Max, who began to sputter. "He said cat flank, not cat food. I swear.....Cat food's on aisle nine, mister."

"Bah!" Jean would pen an epistle to Monsieur Rouses about his employees. The men of Barataria would never be allowed to behave thus.

He found the row of goods with a sign reading "9" above it, and stopped in front of bags and tins of food with images of cats printed on their labels. There were too many, with odd names such as *Meow Mix* and *Little Caesar*. Was the food named after the cat that had been butchered to make it?

None of the tins appeared to be cat-flavored, however.

Jean shrugged. The ungrateful cur Alexander Warin did

not deserve any more of his time. He would find another, more pleasant way to earn Drusilla's favor.

At the front of the store, he walked in and out several times, marveling at how the door knew when he was ready to pass through and opened itself, until he noticed Drusilla standing beside her es-you-vee. Her hands were propped on her hips, and her lips had compressed into a thin line.

Jean hurried to meet her. Apparently, her search for cat had been no more successful than his, but perhaps he might offer her comfort.

Lagniappe: Jean Lafitte–The Man, The Myth, the Undead Pirate

THE LIFE AND DEATH OF the real-life Jean Lafitte is as full of hyperbole and mystery as the man himself, with conflicting stories often perpetuated by Lafitte, depending on his audience.

How closely does the Jean Lafitte of the Sentinels world match up to the real man? Often, developing Jean as a character was a matter of multiple choice.

Here are a few facts and suppositions...

⊕ Jean Lafitte was born about 1780. He claimed at one point to have been born in Bordeaux, France, but he and his brother Pierre at separate times claimed to have been born in Bayonne. For purposes of the series, I chose Bordeaux and the biographical conclusions of historian William C. Davis, who believed Jean to be the youngest son born in 1782 to Pierre Laffite Sr. and his second wife, Marguerite Destell, which would explain the ten-plus-year age difference between Jean and his brother Pierre, born from his father's first marriage.

◈ The family members spelled their name *Laffite*, and Jean and Pierre signed their names with that spelling. The name was Americanized to *Lafitte* during his lifetime, and is seen with that spelling in all of the places named for him. I decided to use the more common version in the novels to avoid having to constantly explain the discrepancy.

◈ Little is known of Jean's early life, but Pierre Lafitte was living in the French colony of San Domingue (now Haiti) by the late 1790s and arrived in New Orleans in 1803, fleeing the Haitian Revolution. Jean is believed to have arrived in New Orleans as captain of his own ship around 1806, when he would have been in his mid-twenties.

◈ There are no existing photographs or drawings of Jean Lafitte. He is described by contemporaries as being six-foot-two (a giant of a man at a time when the average man was five-eight), "well-formed" (ripped), with dark hair, fair skin, and a clean-shaven face. His eye color has been described as dark blue, black, hazel, and even lavender. I stuck with dark blue. He is said to have had small hands and feet; don't even go there!

◈ Jean has been described in historical accounts as having been popular with the ladies, fond of visiting the gambling halls and "quadroon balls" of the city, and with a penchant for dressing well and having impeccable manners. In the

Sentinels novels, Jean is rarely impolite, although his manners often mask other emotions.

⊕ There is no record of Jean ever having married, although several accounts said he had a young mistress in New Orleans, a free woman of color, who bore his only child, a son named Jean Pierre. The little boy and his mother died of yellow fever in New Orleans.

⊕ Along with his impeccable manners and good sense of humor, Jean Lafitte was said to have a hair-trigger temper. I try not to make him too temperamental in the series because I figure, at age 230, give or take a few years, he has learned to bide his time. As an immortal, he has plenty of it, *oui*?

⊕ Jean's first language was French (as was true of New Orleans as a whole during his years there), but he spoke enough English, Spanish, and Italian to make himself understood. His written communications in English are quite literate—and florid. In an 1814 letter to Louisiana Gov. William Claiborne offering his men's cooperation to the Americans in the War of 1812 conflict with England, he describes himself as "the stray sheep, wishing to return to the sheepfold ... worthy to discharge the duties of a good citizen." As DJ would say, "Oh, please."

⊕ Jean was a strong leader and required his men, said to number up to a thousand, to pledge loyalty to him before being allowed to settle in his "kingdom" of Barataria. He was said to be scrupulous about paying his men, dividing profits fairly and paying them on time. He also didn't put up with those who broke his rules, and a man who injured a woman or cheated a colleague might well find himself set adrift in the middle of the Gulf of Mexico with one day's rations.

⊕ Was Jean Lafitte a pirate, or was he—as he insisted—a privateer? And what was the difference? Semantics!

A privateer operated his ships under a letter of marque (a license) from a particular government and could commandeer the ships of a country with which the licensing nation was at war. Jean's ships all carried letters of marque from the Republic of Cartagena (now in Colombia), which was at war with Spain. So he seized every Spanish ship he could get his hands on, took their cargo, and smuggled Spanish goods through New Orleans, undercutting the local merchants and becoming a very rich man.

The merchants were unhappy with this situation, of course, and complained to the governor, who declared Lafitte not a true privateer but a smuggler and pirate—a hanging offense. Did Jean simply buy those licenses so he could skate by piracy charges on a technicality or did he believe himself a true privateer? Potato, potahto.

⊕ Jean Lafitte never lost a duel and fought several. He was adept with both sword and pistol, fueling biographers to surmise that he had at least basic military training as part of his education.

⊕ Jean's house in Barataria was said to be two stories and built in the West Indies style, with cannons on the second floor aimed at possible sites of attack. His men lived in a small seaport village they built down the beach on Grand Terre Island just south of Barataria Bay. In the Sentinels books, I use the name Maison Rouge for his house, but in reality, Maison Rouge was the name of his red-painted house in what is now Galveston, Texas. He moved his operations to what was then called Campeche after leaving Louisiana around 1816 to escape ongoing pressure from the U.S. government. His home in Barataria, as far as I know, did not have a name.

⊕ Of course, in the Sentinels series, Jean Lafitte is immortal. The means and date of his human death are not verified, although there are three prevailing theories:

1) That after leaving Galveston, he settled at Isla Mujeres, northeast of the Yucatan Peninsula, where he died of malaria about 1826;

2) That he began privateering under the marque of Colombia after leaving Galveston, was killed in battle in the early hours of February 5, 1823, and given a military burial at sea in the Gulf of Honduras; and

3) That he changed his name and sailed upriver to Missouri, where he married and lived into his seventies. Historians are split between the first two

theories. They almost unanimously reject the third despite a supposed autobiography discovered in Missouri in the 1940s, which is widely considered a forgery.

RIVALRY

"Rivalry" was one of the first short stories written in the Sentinels world, published for a limited time on my website. It offers our only glimpse so far of Alexander and Jacob Warin's near-sibling rivalry as first cousins growing up in a close-knit family in Picayune, Mississippi, about an hour north of New Orleans. Alex is two years younger than Jake.

In Royal Street, Alex describes Jake as "tough as nails" while Jake describes Alex as a "marshmallow" who hides behind a tough exterior. Are they accurate? That's for you to judge, but this is the story where I came to understand Alex and where his need for order and rules and control originated. Only when one has lost control does one begin to truly value it. Maybe Alex values it to excess...but that's for you (and DJ) to decide.

In terms of a timeline, this story takes place approximately twelve years before the events of Royal Street, when Alex is fifteen and Jake is seventeen.

One

THE PICAYUNE MEMORIAL HIGH School Maroon Tide
expected to have a hell of a football season, and I was
determined to be part of it, sophomore or no sophomore. I
planted my feet on the grass field, brown from the blistering
August sun and dotted with muddy patches from a recent rain,
and watched as the ball arced high into the air and fell in a
graceful spiral toward my chest.

"Sucker!"

My cousin Jake's head butted into my gut, the pigskin
bounced off his helmet, and we crashed, mud splattering our
jerseys. The helmet went flying and I got a mouthful of blood
when my teeth cranked down on my lower lip. By the time he
rolled off me, one shoulder pad stuck out the neck of my shirt.

Folks who say blood tastes like copper are fools. It tasted
like iron and, today, black south Mississippi dirt.

"You think a skinny-assed sophomore's gonna earn a
startin' spot, hotshot?" Jake ripped his own helmet off and
tried to crack me in the head with it, but he'd forgotten my
summer growth spurt. He might be a junior and I might be

skinny, but I was taller than him now and stronger for reasons even I didn't understand. I flipped him easily and shoved his face in the mud hard enough for it to plow through his nose and out his ass. Well, not literally, but that was my goal.

"Warins—Alexander and Jacob. You damn-fool rednecks get to my office now." Coach Bo Dean—we all called him Jethro behind his back—charged toward us with sweat rolling down his face and beady brown eyes screwed up tight.

I rolled off Jake and he sat up, spitting mud on my arm. "Good job, dickface. Now look what you done."

I was still scrambling for a comeback when meaty fists the size of ham hocks grabbed a handful of Jake's blond hair and my dark brown, hauling us to our feet. Jethro was big, strong, and righteously pissed.

"Office. Now, ladies." He shoved us in the direction of the high school gym.

We made the walk of the damned in silence, except Jake kept slipping glances at me out the corner of his eye.

"What?" This was his fault, but I knew he'd figure out a way to pin the blame on me.

"You cut your lip when I clocked you," he mumbled, too low to be heard by Jethro, who stalked a few yards behind us.

"So?"

"So, why ain't it cut now?"

I slid the tip of my tongue to the corner of my mouth and

tasted no fresh blood—just crusty mud.

Shit. Jake wouldn't let it drop, either. He was like a freakin' bulldog. All of a sudden, a fistfight was the least of my worries.

Two

AN HOUR LATER, JAKE and I had our sorry mud-covered butts handed to us by not only Jethro but also our dads, who'd closed down Picayune Hardware for the express purpose of marching to the high school in a united front against their wayward sons.

Tom and Eddie Warin were probably a preview of where Jake and I would end up, Dad tall and broad but mild-tempered, Uncle Eddie shorter and slimmer but hard as a rock. Jake had that banty rooster mentality and wouldn't back down to save his own hide. I considered myself a little more practical, at least until lately.

Lately, I considered myself a freak.

Now I was probably going to be a grounded freak.

Except for an "Alex, yore mama ain't gonna be happy about this," Dad didn't have much to say on the way home. He didn't need to. Mom made up for whatever toughness Dad lacked. She grounded me for two weeks and—worse—subjected me to the I'm-so-disappointed-in-you guilt-trip that might normally have brought me to tears, at least when nobody was looking. That guilt-trip sucked.

I couldn't think about her disappointment, though, or about the ongoing feud with Jake that, by family accounts, began when he knocked me down with a Tonka truck at age four and I, age two, fought back.

Now I was fifteen, with bigger problems. The birds and bees talk I'd gotten from my mortified dad had included lots of halting statements about puberty and hormones and morning hard-ons and the great mystery of girls. I already knew about all that crap from having older brothers.

He didn't tell me a damn thing about healing fast, or being strong, or why I was always hot, or—and here was the real kicker—how I could turn into a dog. And once Jake opened his big fat mouth, the shit would hit the fan.

Three

IT HAPPENED THE FIRST time about three months ago, and Jake had set it off, of course. We'd been fooling around in our granddad Warin's barn, smoking a couple of unfiltered Camels Jake had stolen out of Pop's pocket. The Camel was nasty. I barfed my burger all over a hay bale, and Jake called me a pansy.

Then I got mad and the melting started. My vision changed to muted colors, like in old faded photos or washed-out watercolors, but it was sharp in detail. I smelled everything: the hay, the manure, the vomit, the sickly sweet of Jake's Juicy Fruit gum. By the time I got so hot my insides felt like they were turning to liquid, I'd backed out of the barn door and started to run. Jake's laughter sounded like thunder behind me.

Before I got far into the woods, I changed. It didn't hurt. I just got hot and tingly and then I fell to my hands and knees. Only they weren't hands and knees anymore. They were paws, covered in fur the color of honeysuckle blossoms just before they fall off the vine. My back legs—the dog's back legs—got hung in my pants, and I panicked for a few seconds before finally shaking free.

He was scared that first time. I still can't think of the dog as me; it's just like we share a brain or something. He hid under a thicket of blackberry vines, shaking and whimpering until he fell asleep. I woke up a couple of hours later, naked and covered in scratches, with eyes crusty from crying.

I managed to find my clothes and limp home, slipping in the back and cleaning up before I caught Mom's eye.

I'd asked Pop Warin whether people could turn into animals, figuring that, being an old man who liked to talk, he might be most open to discussing such a thing. He just said they must not be teaching me much in school if a grandson of his was asking such foolish questions. Jake and Donnie, my oldest brother, overheard and began calling me Alexandra.

I never mentioned it again and swore that, whatever it took, I'd be tough and I'd fight. Like today.

My computer screen taunted me as I sat in the bedroom after a solemn, accusatory dinner. Jake had a black eye, Mom said, and since I didn't have a scratch it was obvious who'd picked on whom. I didn't argue, just shoveled in some mashed potatoes and gravy and chicken, and took a chunk of pound cake to my room to help me write my ten-page paper on good sportsmanship for Jethro.

I stared at the computer screen. I had to figure out a way to survive this weird thing that seemed to be happening to me. I was surprised the dog hadn't come out today. But eventually,

I was gonna heal in front of somebody, or Mom would notice my temperature was always about 101 and send me to the doctor, or I was gonna sprout fuzzy ears and a tail in front of somebody. One way or another, this crazy shit was gonna catch up to me.

I peeled off my shirt and looked at myself in the mirror on the back of the door: scrawny chest, messy shock of almost-black hair, dark-brown eyes. I couldn't see the dog in there, staring back. I didn't know how to call him on purpose, and I didn't know how to stop him when he decided to come.

The only thing I could think to do was leave before anybody found out.

Four

I WAITED TILL MIDNIGHT, and even as I stuffed food from the fridge and cabinets into a pillowcase, I could sense The Mutt pacing around behind my ribcage, all anxious and impatient. He wanted out most often when things were tense, or I got angry. Seemed like that had been happening a lot lately.

Mom always rolled her eyes and blamed puberty, but she was lame. I wish it was that simple, but I was pretty sure turning into a dog didn't equate with getting zits.

Easing the front door closed behind me, I shouldered my backpack, got a good grip on the pillowcase of food, and for the first time really thought about what I was doing. Did running away make me a big chicken? Plus, my parents would be scared and no matter how clueless they were, I didn't want them putting my picture on a milk carton or doing one of those crying things on the evening news at the TV station in Hattiesburg. Talk about lame.

I put the stuff down, dug in the backpack for a pen and notebook, and wrote a note.

I'm okay, but I got to leave a while. Don't worry. I'll call when I can.

Love,
Alexander B. Warin

It was pathetic, but at least they'd know I hadn't been kidnapped or murdered and wouldn't put my embarrassing freshman class picture on a milk carton.

I headed out of the neighborhood, moving fast, trying not to think too much, and trying to keep the damned dog inside. I hit the ATM outside a Circle K near the interstate a quarter-mile away, pulling out the $220 I'd made mowing lawns and working at the hardware store over the summer.

Finally, I headed south, into the woods.

I knew where I wanted to go, where I could stay long enough to plan my next move. When Jake and I were kids, we'd wander the woods all around Picayune, playing in prickly brown straw up to our knees and beaning each other with pinecones. We'd found a cave about a mile up Pearl River Ridge, and that's where I'd head tomorrow when the sun rose.

I settled in a thick stand of pine trees and rested my head on the backpack. With the outdoors around me, thick and hot, and the cicadas chirping and animals rustling nearby, The Mutt finally stilled. He seemed relieved to be away, with the pressure off. He knew that, tomorrow, he'd get to run free, whether I wanted him to or not.

Five

IN THE MORNING, I woke to a backpack full of ants and a crick in my neck. I twisted my head from side to side, working out the kinks while I tried to salvage the food. With great regret, I left the cake and leftover chicken behind. I sure was hungry, but not hungry enough to eat ants.

A couple of false starts and an hour later, I found the cave. It was smaller than I remembered, but then again I was last here as a kid and I'd topped six feet on football check-in day last week. Still growing, Dad said.

It would work well enough, just for a few days till I figured out where I wanted to go. I'd always wanted to see the desert, so maybe I'd go to Arizona. I could work odd jobs where I could be outside. As long as nobody got too close, I'd be safe. The Mutt would be safe. 'Cause as much as I wished he wasn't with me, I felt responsible for him. I mean, I could try going to an exorcist or something, but my family's Southern Baptist—they'd probably have me locked up.

The Mutt wouldn't survive being locked up. I had nightmares where I was stuck inside him, instead of him inside me, and a lethal injection of veterinary death drugs was headed his way.

We'd both bite it if one of us died. I don't know how I knew that, but I did.

I felt twitchy, itchy, and hot as I set up a little camp in the cave. I knew what that meant, and for the first time ever I stripped down, relaxed my mind and body, and let The Mutt come out without fighting him. He trotted to the opening of the cave and lay there for a while, looking around with my brain running in his head and his senses filtering through my mind. It was some more weird shit.

His vision was amazing, even with the pale colors. Every leaf, every pine branch stood out from the next. The smells were intense, from the peanut butter jar in the backpack to something a dead squirrel or rabbit, maybe rotting underneath the carpet of pine straw.

For the next three days, me and The Mutt learned to live together. I'd eat breakfast, get undressed, and let him run through the woods all day. He found a stream, and I hoped it wasn't so full of fertilizer runoff and animal crap it would kill us. The Mutt would come back to the cave at night, and turn back into me so I could eat and sleep. Even he seemed to realize hands were convenient things to have.

By the third day, most of the food was gone, but he caught a squirrel and killed it. I didn't have anything to start a fire, though, and I couldn't bring myself to eat it raw. So I went to sleep hungry, and left the squirrel outside the cave. In the morning it was gone, and I didn't want to think about what might've got it, or if The Mutt had eaten it without me knowing.

Six

MR. JONES SHOWED UP on day five during a driving rainstorm. I knew it was the fifth day because I'd been scratching off the days in the dirt like castaways do in the movies, or inmates counting the time until their prison jig is up. Mine wouldn't ever be up, not with The Mutt around, and it made me think of what that dog had cost me.

I wondered what my mom and dad were doing, if the sheriff was hunting for me, what they thought had happened. I wondered if my brothers were glad I was gone. Donnie had probably already taken my computer. Mom always wanted a sewing room. Maybe she'd already packed my stuff away, taken down my New Orleans Saints posters, and filled my room with fabric and thread.

The hot pressure of tears built behind my eyeballs, and I thought about seeing if The Mutt would come out just to spare me the humiliation of crying like a baby. Wouldn't Jake just love to see that?

I should go to New Orleans before I worried about Arizona. I could hitch a ride south—it was only 50 miles—and fall in with some of those people of ill repute Mom said lived there. All those restaurants must throw out a lot of food, and I was awfully hungry. If I went much longer without eating more than a spoonful of peanut butter every now and then, The Mutt would convince me to eat some raw, dead thing.

I'd kept him inside all day while it rained, and the cave was steamy and damp. I curled up in the back using my grimy shirt as a pillow, staring out at the green, dripping branches, watching rainwater pool at the mouth of the cave. It had to have rained more than an inch already and it hadn't brought a lick of coolness to the air.

"You are in one sorry state, son."

I scrambled to my feet, jerked out of my doze, and stared at the man standing in the mouth of the cave— a black man wearing a gray t-shirt and faded overalls. I'd never seen him before, and working summers at Warin Hardware I knew most of the farmers around here at least by sight.

My throat felt dry and I cleared it before I could speak. "Who are you?"

"Reggie Jones." He held out a long-fingered hand for me to shake, and his grip was strong. The hand wasn't work-roughened like that of a farmer. "I been looking for you, son. Don't 'preciate you making me track you through these woods in the rain."

He gave me a once-over and peered around me at my backpack. "Don't seem like you been eatin' too good up here."

I decided I'd better take the offensive and let him know I

wouldn't be pushed around. "Look, mister, you aren't making me go home. Unless you got Sheriff Williamson with you, you might as well go back wherever you came from. Forget you saw me."

I clenched my fists, figuring I could punch him a time or two if I had to.

He smiled, then grinned, and finally laughed. Even slapped his knee before sitting cross-legged on the floor of the cave to pull off his wet shoes. Not the reaction I'd been shooting for.

"I'm hopin' once you hear what I got to say, you'll go on home." He poured some water out of a heavy leather shoe, then set the pair neatly side by side.

I stared at him, trying to figure out who he was. I knew who he wasn't. He wasn't a farmer from Picayune, Mississippi—or anywhere else, Mississippi, for that matter. His accent wasn't right, for one thing, and his hands were too soft. And farmers around Picayune, Mississippi, didn't wear overalls in late August. It was too damned hot.

He watched me watching him. "You're a smart one, maybe. Got some brains workin' in there. That's good, because you got some decisions to make."

Yeah, like how to get rid of this guy. When to leave for New Orleans. Where to go once I got to the big city. Whether it would hurt me to eat dirt, and if it would be filling. I had a feeling that wasn't what he meant. "What kind of decisions?"

"Your animal, boy. What is it?"

The Mutt bristled uneasily inside me.

"I don't know what you're talking about." How did he know? What did he know? Had he been watching me?

The rain fell steadily outside the cave as we eyed each other in silence. Finally, he sighed and rose to his feet. I was still thinking about how he'd gotten up from the ground awful easy for an old guy when he shimmered a little and seemed to disintegrate in front of me.

My breath hitched and I backed against the cave wall, staring at the small red fox shaking itself and stepping with almost dainty white feet from the puddled overalls. The Mutt growled and paced inside me, and I fought that hot, melting feeling.

Reggie Jones was like me. And, somehow, he'd found me.

As suddenly as the fox had appeared, Mr. Jones took his place again. A shimmer, a slight movement of air, and he stood there. I knew it was rude, not to mention unmanly-like, to stare at a naked guy, but I couldn't peel my eyes away. He calmly slipped back into his clothes and resumed his seat on the floor of the cave as if nothing crazy had happened.

"So, I ask you again, boy. What's your animal?"

I slid down the cave wall to the ground, wondering when I was gonna wake up and hoping it would be soon. "A dog," I said softly. I couldn't believe I'd admitted it, and how calm said dog had become inside me. "I call him The Mutt."

Mr. Jones's booming laugh echoed around the cave. "That's just disrespectful, son." He reached in the bib of his overalls, pulled out two Payday candy bars, and tossed one to me. "We need to talk about what you and The Mutt are going to do. Got plans, do you?"

I wasn't ready to share my plans, such as they were. "How did you know about me? How did you find me? Did my parents send you?"

He took a big bite out of the candy bar and pointed to his nose while he chewed. "No, your parents don't know what you are, and they don't need to know. Those of us who turn into some canine or another—dog, fox, whatever—we got that good sense of smell. I tracked you here pretty easy."

I ate the candy bar in three bites and, in a burst of sugar-fueled courage, asked the big question. "What are we?" I had an epiphany. "Are we like werewolves?"

I wanted to take the words back as soon as they were out. Stupid.

Mr. Jones didn't laugh, and that scared me even more. "Naw, not were-anythings. Werewolves got all that nasty bone-crunching and moon schedule thing going down. Painful, I hear. We're shapeshifters, boy. We change when we want. It's a kind of magic."

I rubbed my eyes, tired and confused and obviously sitting in a cave with a damn fool. Except I'd seen the fox. Maybe I was hallucinating from starvation.

"You got any more candy?"

He grinned, his teeth flashing in the dim light of the cave. "You need to go home, boy, if you want to eat. Surely you got more questions than whether I got another Payday on me."

Tears threatened again. I was acting like a flipping girl. "I don't know where to start."

Mr. Jones sighed. "Okay, Alexander, I'll just give you the basics."

I stared at him. He hadn't used my name before.

"Don't be giving me the evil eye over there. The wizards keep up with all the magical folk in the world. They have their ways, and all you need to know right now is they sent me to help you sort things out. Somebody back in your family tree might have been a shapeshifter and you got the lucky gene, or sometimes it just happens for reasons nobody knows. You're how old now, about fifteen?"

I nodded, my tongue glued to the top of my mouth.

"You changed early, which is why we weren't ready for you. Shifters usually don't start changing till seventeen or eighteen." He pulled a handkerchief out of his pocket and wiped the sweat off his face. "Anyway, you gotta decide if you want to keep this gift or let it go."

Let it go? For the first time in months, I felt an ounce of hope. The world might be full of possibility again. Maybe I could have a life. "It's not a gift. I don't want it. How do I get rid of it?"

He shook his head. "Don't be so hasty, son. You need to think about it."

"No." I was adamant. "I want The Mutt gone. If you can do it, I want you to. Now."

Mr. Jones studied me a long couple of minutes. Finally, he

leaned against the wall of the cave and turned his head the other way, watching the rain and talking so softly I had to strain to hear. "You're just scared now because you don't know how to control it, but the animal is part of you. If you practice, he'll come and go when you want him to. You'll live a longer life than most folks. You won't get sick. You'll heal fast from just about anything."

He turned his head to look at me. "You'll be physically strong—really strong—if you put some effort into it."

"What good is it?" I couldn't understand why he'd want me to keep this curse. Why he'd kept his. Maybe no one had given him a choice, or he'd made the wrong one.

"You have to answer that one for yourself, son. Just think about it. I'll find you again in a couple of days. You decide to keep Mr. Mutt, then I'll hang around and show you how to control him. And you're too skinny. Start lifting weights —fill out that scrawny stringbean of a body. Be careful with contact sports. If you get yourself hurt and heal too fast, that'll draw attention, so don't get hurt. Eat lots of protein. You get out of school and want to work with others like us, we'll take care of it."

My head spun from too much information that didn't make sense. "What kind of work?" My voice sounded distant and weak, and then I thought of something else. "What do you mean wizards? There are wizards? And werewolves?"

"We'll talk about that after you decide," he said, and rose

to his feet. "I'll catch up with you."

Mr. Jones walked out of the cave, back into the rain.

I didn't follow him.

Seven

THE RAINS HAD ENDED by the time I got up the next morning, and I pulled on my grimy clothes with every intention of hitching a ride to New Orleans. Instead, I ended up near the high school, watching from behind the concession stand as a few of the older boys threw the ball, just fooling around and killing time. No practice on Saturday.

I felt a million years old, standing there and watching them. Their world had been taken away from me, unless I decided to take it back.

Jake and two of his classmates, the Gibson brothers, ran over to the stands nearest me, not realizing I was there. Jimmy pulled a pack of Marlboros from his pocket and passed it around. Jake lit up with them, and they all leaned back and watched the other boys gradually leave the field till no one was left but them.

The air had a touch of coolness in it finally, a promise of the coming fall. They'd all be playing football in a couple of weeks, and seeing who could hit third base with the Holcombe sisters. They'd be normal kids. I wasn't sure where I'd be, but my life was looking real different unless I got rid of The Mutt.

He hadn't stirred since Mr. Jones had left, like he suspected his days were numbered and maybe I'd change my mind if he behaved himself. I wasn't sure why I hadn't made the decision. Wasn't sure why I'd let Reggie Jones walk out of that cave without removing this curse.

Wasn't sure how I could care about The Mutt when he was screwing up my life. But somehow, he'd started to feel as if he were part of me.

A sudden movement from the stands jerked me back to the present. Derrick Gibson had shoved Jake, and Jimmy had thrown down his cig and stood with his fists clenched. They were talking low and I couldn't hear them, but the Gibsons were bad news. Dad always told me to stay away from them, and said Jake'd end up in trouble if he kept hanging with them.

Once Uncle Eddie had said the same thing to Jake, it pretty much guaranteed he'd try to make Derrick and Jimmy Gibson his best friends.

Jimmy threw the first punch. He was bigger and taller than Jake, and meaner. Jake beat him in pure stubbornness, though, so he fought back, and they all tumbled off the stands to the ground.

By the time Derrick had Jake in a headlock and Jimmy started throwing punches to his ribs, The Mutt had begun to pace. He wanted out, but he seemed to be waiting for me to give him permission.

A smash to the face sent a spray of blood flying from Jake's mouth. They were beating the tar out of him and didn't look ready to stop anytime soon. I knew Jake; he wouldn't stop fighting until they half-killed him, or worse.

I closed my eyes and called to The Mutt, begging him to come. The melting started before I could finish the thought. We shucked off the clothes and tore into Jimmy Gibson from the side, knocking him flat and snapping at arms and legs with our teeth. We could kill him, I realized with a wave of satisfaction. We stood over him, panting, and took in his wide eyes and his shouts for help. Derrick had backed away, too afraid to come near us.

It was the most power I'd ever felt in my life, and I liked it.

With a deep growl, I lowered my mouth to Jimmy's neck and bit. Not deep. Not enough to draw blood. Just enough to scare him so bad he pissed all over himself.

Then I backed away and snarled at Derrick.

They ran without looking back, and I turned my attention to Jake. He tried to get to his feet but fell back and tried to scoot away from me. I lay down and whined, trying to show him he didn't have to be afraid of me, although some part of me liked the idea I could scare him.

He smiled, showing the dimples all the girls went apeshit over, sending a fresh trickle of blood trailing off his chin from his busted lip. Funny how this whole thing had started with a busted lip, and now here we were again.

"Hey, furball, you saved me." He held out a hand, palm up,

and clicked his tongue for me to come to him.

I rose slowly and walked to sit beside him, reaching my head up to lick his face. He stroked my fur—The Mutt's fur—and sniffled. Godalmighty, he was crying. I whined and licked his face again.

I hadn't thought Jake knew how to cry. It was a revelation.

"S'okay, furball. Just been a bad week, you know? Jethro's been on my ass all week, and my cousin Alex ran away and I think it was my fault. Man, I miss that big dumb shit."

He wiped the tears off his cheeks and grunted as he used me for leverage to regain his feet.

"Come on, dog. I gotta figure out how to get cleaned up before my mom or dad see me." He started back across the field in the direction of his house, but I stayed where I was, watching him leave. He turned once to look at me, but when I didn't move he waved and continued on his way.

Eight

I GOT GROUNDED FOR six months, or maybe for life; Mom couldn't make up her mind. She'd been shoving food at me since I showed up on the front doorstep, dirty and hungry. I was obviously one of those troubled youths she'd read about in the newspaper, she said. I'd have to talk to a counselor in Hattiesburg, there being no such thing in Picayune and the ones in New Orleans were probably members of the mob or, worse, Catholic.

Jake had punched me in the shoulder hard enough to cause a bruise when he'd come to see if I was really home. I didn't hit back, just smiled and told him I'd missed him too. It shut him up.

There's a new guy working at Warin Hardware now, helping stock shelves and waiting on customers since Jake and I are back in school, which ended the supply of free labor. His name is Reggie Jones, and Dad says he's a quiet, polite man and is glad I'm spending lots of time with him on weekends, learning to fish.

I'm learning a lot of things. And yeah, there are werewolves and wizards.

SWAMP RATS

"Swamp Rats" was created from two deleted early scenes from Elysian Fields, *and originally featured DJ and Jake Warin rather than DJ and Alex. It was adapted into a flash-fiction short in 2013 under a different name. Although they're mentioned a few times in other stories and are seen in the standalone novelette* Chenoire *(written as Susannah Sandlin), weregators make their only appearance in the Sentinels world in this story. Timewise, "Swamp Rats" takes place shortly after the events of* River Road.

"HERE'S THE DEAL, JUST so we're clear." I planted my five-four frame in front of weregator chieftain Zeke Marchand, who was built roughly like a giant water oak with leathery skin instead of bark.

Behind me skulked the slimmer, shorter merman Denis Villere. The mer had a Napoleon complex—he was vertically challenged, arrogant, and mean as a rabid swamp rat. He probably had the same opinion of me, and I didn't care.

"The Villeres can live in the area east of Bayou Teche," I said. "The Marchands live west. You know the boundaries."

To me, the swamps in St. Martin Parish, southwest of Baton Rouge, formed a maze: every bend in the bayou, every whiff of dark water, every caw of cormorant or clack of pelican added to the confusion. I could get lost out here in a heartbeat. Wizards didn't come with built-in GPS. Pity.

Zeke and Denis ignored me while they sized each other up, probably to decide who'd be able to eat whom the fastest. Gauging by his size, Zeke was a big bull gator; I'd seen Denis's mer form, a smallish dolphin.

Both had were-shifter strength, and Denis would beat Zeke

on stamina. I'd still bet my next year's salary on the gator. One could only stretch the laws of physics so far.

"Good." I looked from Zeke to Denis, neither of whom had uttered as much as a squawk. "I'll consider your silence an agreement."

In my peripheral vision, I saw today's backup, Alex Warin, slip out of his big truck and pull the handgun from his shoulder holster. He'd spent the past two hours pretending not to listen while I negotiated the treaty. Not the most glamorous assignment we'd ever had, but sentinels can't be choosy. Plus, the Villere merclan had been a pain in our asses ever since I'd had to run them out of Plaquemines Parish. They'd poached on another clan's territory and withheld pertinent information in a preternatural murder investigation.

"I ain't agreed to nothing." Denis assumed what I called the *merman stance*—hands on hips and legs spread wide, the better to stay upright when standing aboard a storm-tossed ship. Most of the South Louisiana mers and weregators mainstreamed as commercial fishermen. "We ain't getting' nothing good out of this deal."

Boots making only a whisper of sound among the squawks of swamp hens and rustling of reeds, Alex moved behind Denis, not breathe-down-his-neck close but in a position to move fast if the need to shoot something with special bullets arose. Although if this scene really went to hell, he'd shift into a big golden dog the size of a small pony.

At that point I'd have a monster dog, a monster fish, and a monster gator on my hands, because I was the only thing in this little isolated bend of Bayou Teche who couldn't turn into something bigger and badder than herself. I did, however, have a vicious staff of elven origin, and I knew how to use it. Well, if it didn't require much accuracy.

"If you can't respect our territory, we got problems, shrimp-face." Zeke took a step toward Denis, hands bunched into fists. He brushed me aside and went chest-to-nose with the mer.

Holy crap. Couldn't anything be simple? Using the staff was a last resort, so I pulled a spare distraction charm from my jeans pocket, flipped off the top of the vial, and slung the contents at a nearby cypress knee sticking out of the watery ground. It exploded into an impressive cloud of smoke and flame, but unlike the fire I could shoot with the staff, it wouldn't really burn anything.

"I-yi-yi." Zeke stepped back with a sharp intake of breath. Denis's nose crinkled as if he smelled a bad fish.

I threw in some bravado. "Let's work this out, unless you want another demonstration of what happens when you don't cooperate."

While Zeke and Denis pondered the stump covered in faux-flame, Alex holstered his gun, gave me a sexy grin, and returned to the truck. He shook his head, dark hair curling over the top of his collar. Glad I amused him.

I poked the elven staff in Zeke's chest, grinding my teeth

to avoid whining from too much movement. Under my red sweater, I had a midriff wrapped so tightly in elastic tape I might as well be mummified, thanks to merman CPR from a recent case. Different merman, though; Denis would've let me drown in a heartbeat.

"Zeke, your family is not to eat any of the Villeres, even if you're in gator form and Denis flips his wimpy little fin between your jaws." Which was, frankly, more self-control than I'd be able to exercise. "In exchange, you're getting twice the territory you previously had."

His reptilian gaze (literally) slid over me, and he gave a slow blink of gold-flecked green eyes. "No disrespect, Miss DJ, but if he flips any damn thing in my jaws, it's gonna get bit." His voice somehow managed to both rumble and slither. Not a pleasant combination. "And dere ain't gonna be no evidence. He just"—Zeke snapped fingers the size of jumbo crab claws— "gonna disappear, him and his whole clan."

I sighed and turned to Denis. "Well? You know your options."

The wizards' Congress of Elders, the ruling body for prete behavior in the modern world, had given Denis a choice. He could move his whining, self-entitled family here to the eastern edge of the Atchafalaya Basin, or relocate out of the human world and into the Beyond.

Sort of a prete witness protection program, without the protection. I had no sympathy for him. His nasty little mother had once threatened to boil me for dinner.

"Told you he wouldn't agree, you stupid wizard. Gators got 'bout as much honor as wizards, which be none." Denis sidestepped me and lunged for Zeke, never mind the weregator had at least a hundred pounds and more than a foot of height on him. The mer stood five-seven or five-eight of wiry sun-browned muscle—no match for a guy who turned into a twelve-foot, leather-clad eating machine.

I thrust the staff toward Denis, but hesitated before powering it up. I wasn't sure how to wield this weapon gently. I'd set him on fire or flat-out kill him. With me and this ancient relic the elves called Mahout and I called Charlie, there was no middle ground. I either held two feet of inert polished wood or I wielded the magical equivalent of a firing squad. With real fire.

Finally, ignoring the stabbing pain in my midsection, I raised the staff over my head with both hands and beaned Denis with it. When in doubt, improvise.

"Shit! That the best you got, you stupid little girl?" He grabbed the tip of the staff and yanked, but I wouldn't let go. With Zeke's gruff laughter providing a soundtrack, we tugged back and forth, each jerk sending hot pokers of pain through my ribcage. Maybe I *should* set the jackass on fire.

A loud pop stopped us in mid-tug. Alex sat on the hood of his shiny black Range Rover, managing to look bored even as he pointed his pistol toward the clear late-autumn sky. The shot echoed through the centuries-old cypress swamp, and in its wake, silence.

Denis let go, robbing me of the chance to give him the beat-down he deserved.

"Let's start over." I clutched the staff so tightly red sparks flew out the end, which made both the men swear and back away. Sweet. "Zeke, you okay with the new agreement?"

"My family'll keep our part of it," he rumbled. "Which means right now, he is on my side of da bayou."

"Yeah, we okay, like you give us a choice. Witch." With a final evil eye in my direction, Denis turned and stalked to his motorcycle.

"Did you just call me a witch? Seriously?" My dislike of this guy rose higher than the Spanish moss topping the trees. Witches were vastly inferior to wizards.

He cranked, revved, and fishtailed out of the small clearing without a backward glance. That mer gave *got some bad fish* a whole new meaning.

I took a deep breath and shook off his negative vibes. Despite my morning grounding ritual to avoid absorbing his hostility, I still pulled in some of his emotional energy. Welcome to the world of an empath.

"Thanks, Zeke." I tucked the staff into its makeshift thigh holster.

"We all good, wizard. Got us more huntin' grounds." Zeke wrapped huge, leathery fingers around mine in some approximation of a handshake, and slithered off to hunt whatever weregators hunted.

I didn't want to know.

DANGER: CURVES AHEAD

"Danger: Curves Ahead" was a flash-fiction short written in 2013 and originally published on the Bittersweet Enchantment blog in August of that year. It features wizard sentinel DJ Jaco and her significant-something-or-other, Alex Warin. DJ likes chocolate; Alex likes beer. They have a bet to see who gives in first, and DJ wins. She might have cheated. Timewise, "Danger: Curves Ahead" takes place between River Road *and* Elysian Fields.

ALEX WARIN BALKED AT the soggy parking lot of Elmwood Center, frowning at the strip mall in front of him and ignoring a gaggle of elderly, white-haired women in yoga pants, purple t-shirts, and bright red hats tottering past to get out of the rain. "This wasn't part of the deal."

The sign on the door in front of us read *Curves for Women*.

I tried to stifle a grin from deep inside the hood of my yellow rain slicker. I'm sure the gloat shone through, however, as I grabbed his wrist and tugged him toward the door. "I won the bet. You broke down and drank a beer before I even had a whiff of chocolate. That means I pick the gym."

Eight solid days of rain had turned our jogging path in New Orleans' Audubon Park into a mud-filled trench worthy of WWE pit wrestling. This was our compromise.

"DJ, I know you put that six-pack of Turbo Dog in my refrigerator." Alex's deep baritone developed a somewhat canine whine. "You played dirty."

Damn straight. Like that monstrous Hershey bar on my coffee table had arrived via pixie courier.

I pushed open the Curves door, pulling him behind me like a six-foot-three-inch toddler with a case of the Terrible Twos.

He shook water out of his hair to annoy me, but I was having too much fun at the idea of Mr. Macho doing Zumba with members of the Senior Red Hat Society of Greater New Orleans.

I'd called ahead to make sure they'd let him in, and knew for a fact that the group, whose minimum age was sixty-five, met for rigorous senior-adult butt-shaking every Tuesday morning and would love to have a virile young man to ogle.

When we reached the front counter, I released Alex's wrist and gave him a warning glare not to bolt. I had my elven staff inside my rain slicker. Not that zapping him in a room full of crimson-hatted matrons would be worth all the trouble it would cause. My Green Congress wizarding skills could handle it with the memory-erasure charms I had in my bag, but I hated to be brought up on human-elder-abuse charges.

"I'm DJ Jaco," I told the woman behind the counter. "I talked to you earlier about my friend Alex coming in for a workout this morning?"

The perky brunette behind the counter looked past me at said friend, and I swear she purred. "I'm sure the ladies won't mind if he joins them." She added as an afterthought, "and you too, of course."

"Of course." I glanced over my shoulder at Alex, who'd straightened his shoulders and assumed his I'm-hot-sex-on-two-legs-and-I-know-it expression. It involved a slow smile and a sultry gaze from eyes the color of the uneaten candy bar that had gone from the coffee table to my purse as soon as I was sure he'd taken the beer bait.

The man was shameless.

Nikki, as the brunette's name tag identified her, elbowed past me and slid a hand through Alex's conveniently crooked arm. "C'mon, hon. Your friend said you were shy but we ladies won't bite." The purr returned. "Well, not much."

Alex looked over his shoulder and gave me a smirk I recognized too well. He had a plan. If it involved shedding clothes and shifting into his pony-sized dog form, I didn't care what elders got abused. He was getting zapped with the staff.

Suddenly, I realized my appetite for exercise had been replaced by my taste for chocolate. Keeping my rain slicker on in case I needed quick access to the staff, I dug the chocolate bar out of my bag and leaned against the counter.

Alex had been surrounded by at least a half-dozen women in hats that ranged from ruby-red straw with fake daisies around the brim to a burgundy felt fedora with rain-bedraggled feathers sagging in its band.

"Okay, everyone, let's line up and do some Zumba!" Nikki took her place at the front of the group, and they all shuffled into two neat rows, with Alex at the end. I swear the woman next to him, every bit of five-foot-two and eighty if she was a day, pinched his ass, and he laughed.

If I even admired that ass too long, he'd tell me to stop leering. God knows what he'd do if I pinched it. Talk about a double standard.

"I think Alex should stand up front with you, Nikki!"

shouted the Pincher. "He'll inspire us to work harder!"

Ha. He'd never do it. He'd turn Neanderthal on them, growl a few times, and we could get out of here. I'd even admit it was a stupid idea.

"Sure thing." He swaggered to the head of the class and gave me a long, pointed look before grasping the bottom of his black t-shirt and pulling it over his head. "Need to get out of this wet shirt, though."

Every woman in the room sighed.

Except me. I took an enormous bite of chocolate and chewed like a goat. At least until the deafening Latin music began, followed by various degrees of hip swiveling. At least half the Red Hats were avidly watching one particular set of hips in black jogging pants.

Not me. I jerked my hood up, stomped unnoticed out the door, and sloshed through the parking lot toward Burger King. There was a chocolate shake with my name on it.

LAGNIAPPE: A SENTINELS BIBLIOGRAPHY

W ANT TO KNOW MORE about the stories behind the stories?
Check out some of my favorite references.

One Dead in Attic, by Chris Rose

A collection of *Times-Picayune* newspaper columns written
from New Orleans by reporter Chris Rose in the days and
months immediately after Hurricane Katrina. "One Dead in
Attic" refers to a sign spray-painted on a house that Rose rode
past on his bike through the deserted, ruined city. Powerful
stuff, even now. (Simon & Schuster, 2007)

The Great Deluge: Hurricane Katrina, New Orleans, and the Mississippi Gulf Coast, by Douglas Brinkley

This massive book, released only a year after the storm, is part
journalism, part history, part emotion. Of the many books
released later about Katrina, this book, along with the Chris
Rose columns (above), present the clearest picture of the
locals' perception of events as they happened. (William

Morrow, 2006)

Satchmo: My Life in New Orleans, by Louis Armstrong.
An autobiography by the jazz man himself. (Ulan, 2012; originally published prior to 1923)

The Pirates Laffite: The Treacherous World of the Corsairs of the Gulf, by William C. Davis
Probably the definitive history of Jean and Pierre Lafitte, copiously researched and footnoted. (Harcourt, 2005)

Patriotic Fire: Andrew Jackson and Jean Lafitte at the Battle of New Orleans, by Winston Groom
A wonderful account of the dynamics between two very different men forced to work together to save New Orleans from the English in 1815. (Knopf, 2006)

Lafitte the Pirate, by Lyle Saxon
Originally published in 1930, this is not considered the most accurate Jean Lafitte biography, but it is certainly one of the most entertaining. (Pelican, 1989)

Voodoo in New Orleans, by Robert Tallant
Written in 1946, the book is both florid and fascinating. (Macmillan, 1946; Pelican, 1983)

The Encyclopedia of Magical Herbs and *The Encyclopedia of Crystal, Gem, and Metal Magic,* both by Scott Cunningham

Great references on the supernatural properties generally associated with common and not-so-common items. Most of DJ's charms and potions were developed from these sources. (Llewellyn, 1985, herbs; Llewellyn, 1988, gems)

The Music of Zachary Richard

Louisiana Cajun artist, author, and singer-songwriter extraordinaire. His music, both in English and French, has formed my playlist for the series. The song "La Ballade de Jean Batailleur" (from the album *Cap Enragé*) particularly influenced the direction in which I took Jake Warin's character arc, and the vampire club L'Amour Sauvage came from a line in his song "Un Coeur Fidèle" (which appears on the album *Coeur Fidèle*). Find more at http://www.zacharyrichard.com.

INTERVENTION

As we've seen, the rivalry between Alex Warin and his cousin Jake is legendary. We don't know a lot about Jake's experiences between his Marine Corps duty in Afghanistan, where he was injured, and his life when he meets DJ. We know he owns a Bourbon Street bar called the Green Gator and that he's had problems with alcohol. In "Intervention," we'll learn a bit more about Jake, about Alex, and that their love for each other runs as deep as their rivalry (just don't tell them!). In timeline terms, this story takes place a year or two before Royal Street.

One

FAMILY COULD BE SUCH a pain in the ass. Jake was cooling his jets in a New Orleans jail. Again.

Ending the call with his mother, Alexander Warin massaged the residual throbbing in his temples and squinted through the slats of his living room blinds. His soon-to-be-ex girlfriend stalked around his car clutching a rumpled piece of paper. He recognized the "Dear Cindy" letter on FBI letterhead he'd slipped under her door after his early-morning run.

It had been a chickenshit move, but lately she'd gotten clingy and possessive. He'd never promised hearts and flowers. If the woman wanted a lapdog, she needed to date an accountant, or a vet.

He clenched his jaw muscles as she tested the lock on the driver's-side door of his black Mercedes convertible, polished to its habitual gloss. If she as much as *thought* about scraping her car keys across his custom paint job, she would see how handcuffs felt when she was fully dressed.

Hands on her hips, she stared at the front of his condo a few long moments before sticking up the middle finger of each hand in the classic gesture for things they'd already done upside down and sideways. Then she climbed back in her sissy little SUV and left skid marks on his driveway.

He grinned and let the slats flap shut. Perfect.

Alex returned to his bedroom, throwing clothes in the suitcase he'd begun packing halfway through his mom's call. Norma Warin was not a force to be denied, and if she said drive to New Orleans and get your cousin out of jail, well, he'd be spending his long weekend dealing with Jake.

After a quick recon to make sure the newly liberated Cindy wasn't lying in wait, Alex took his black overnighter, put it in the trunk, and climbed in for the four-hour drive from Jackson to New Orleans. He punched the key into the ignition, paused, and pulled it back out.

Jake was in trouble, and Alex wouldn't be a welcome sight. The cousins' rivalry was legendary in their hometown of Picayune, Mississippi. Plus, New Orleans was a festering boil on the ass of crime—both human and preternatural. He needed weapons.

Twenty minutes later, he hit I-55 heading south, his bag sitting on the back floorboard so his armory would fit in the trunk. He'd shoved his Tracker, a wizard-issued device to trace preternatural energy, into his pocket. His baby—a big, solid Colt .45 with custom grips and a barrel modified for specialized ammo—rested in a shoulder holster beneath his black sports coat.

The serious firepower was in the trunk. He might be an enforcer for the wizarding world's Congress of Elders, but Alex Warin ranked a few human foes right up there on the danger scale with werewolves and goblins. One never knew what might show up in New Orleans spoiling for a fight, including pissed-off ex-Marine cousins.

Two

ALEX EASED THE CAR through the congested streets of downtown New Orleans and made his way through progressively seedier neighborhoods till he found the mammoth Orleans Parish Courthouse. Behind it sat the blocky parish jail. He flashed his FBI badge at the bored officer manning the lot next to Central Lockup, and wedged the car into a narrow spot beside an overflowing dumpster noisy with flies.

That no one in the family had the nerve to drive the hour from Picayune to pick up Jake after his mandatory forty-eight hours in lockup told boatloads about their frustration. Jake had seemed better lately, more like the man he'd been before Afghanistan. Now this. Second DUI. Working full-time at the bar. No interest in anything—well, except the "New Orleans floozy" his mom said Jake had taken up with.

Norma Warin's idea of what constituted a fallen woman was broad and wide, however, so Alex didn't put much stock in it.

He stared at the dumpster, plotting a strategy. He wouldn't

coddle Jake. That was part of the problem. Ever since the remnants of his Marine unit had limped back from Afghanistan, the family had tiptoed around him.

Alex didn't tiptoe. The wizards responsible for keeping the borders between the modern world and the preternatural world Beyond had recruited him early, trained him for their preternatural task force with an FBI front, and taught him to fight hard and shoot fast. If he could handle the monsters normal folks didn't know about, he could damned well handle his cousin's internal monsters.

Plus, if it came to a fist fight, he'd win. Jake was more likely to play dirty, but Alex was taller and had plenty of muscle.

Central Lockup was hopping, even early on a Friday afternoon, and after making sure Jake's legal ducks were aligned, Alex settled against the lime sherbet-colored cinderblock walls and watched the flotsam and jetsam of New Orleans' underbelly ebb and flow.

A door slammed in the back of the building, clanging metal, and Jake headed toward him down a narrow hallway alongside a man whose appearance Alex assessed with a practiced eye: African-American, neatly dressed, a couple inches shorter than Jake, so about five-nine, bland business suit. Too rumpled and off-the-rack to be a lawyer; Alex guessed NOPD detective. Why would Jake rate a detective escort—unless he was in more trouble than a simple DUI?

His eyes shifted to his cousin and his stomach flipped. Holy shit. He hadn't seen Jake in three months, and the change was marked. Jake's frame, always hard and steel-plated wiry compared to Alex's bulk, looked gaunt, and the limp from Afghanistan was more pronounced. He'd torn up both legs with a tumble from a cliff that had probably saved his life, but no amount of surgery could help get him back in track-running shape. His expression was frayed and exhausted—until he spotted Alex leaning against the wall.

A careful mask of insolence settled into place. "Well, I know things are bad now," he drawled. "The family *federale* has been sent to deal with poor, screwed-up Jacob."

His voice carried across the room, barely rating a blip on the collective apathy of lawyers, cops, and detainees.

The detective steered him toward the line at the window to be processed out, then headed toward Alex. "I'm Ken Hachette." He stuck out a hand.

Alex gave himself a mental slap. He should have realized who this was: Jake's Marine buddy and co-owner of their French Quarter bar, the Green Gator—and a cop. They'd never met, but Alex had heard good things about the guy. Straight arrow. Sober and serious. The kind of friend Jake needed.

"You're a detective now?"

Ken nodded, his expression somber. "Homicide."

A chill of fear ran through Alex. "Damn it. Who'd he kill?"

Ken's laugh was humorless. "Nobody, at least not that I know of. I'm just here to make sure he gets out of lockup without his smartass mouth making him a permanent resident. Hope you can talk some sense into him."

Yeah, good luck with that. Alex and Jake had been knocking the crap out of each other since four-year-old Jake had beaned two-year-old Alex with a Tonka truck. A big growth spurt in high school gave Alex a size advantage but Jake made up for it with a wide streak of ornery. Thing was, Alex knew about the preternatural world and how easily things could fall apart without rules and order. Jake didn't know about pretes, and despite his military training, rules and order weren't his favorite words.

Jake had reached the processing window, and Alex shook his head. "Give me the short version."

"Not sure," Ken said, crossing his arms. "I thought he was doing good. Has a lot of pain in that right leg, but he's been doing a great job at the Gator. Then he got this new girlfriend about a month ago and..." he shook his head. "She's bad news. I swear the problem starts and ends with her."

Maybe Norma had been right. "Who's the chick?"

Ken's answer was interrupted by Jake's sudden appearance at his elbow. "Hachette-man, I see you've met Buffy." Jake grinned, the dimples and shaggy blond hair the same as always but no life in his amber-colored eyes.

Ken raised an eyebrow. "Buffy?"

"Well, hell, look at him. He's the family specimen. Big Buff Federal Agent. A real man's man."

Alex fought to keep an Elvis snarl from curling his upper lip. "This isn't the place, Jake. Let's go."

In an instant, Jake deflated. He clapped Ken on the shoulder and pushed the door open ahead of him. He let it slam in Alex's face.

On his way out, Alex looked back as Ken tapped him on the arm and handed him a business card. "Call me."

Three

THEY SPENT A HALF hour of mostly silence on the drive to the French Quarter, where Jake lived in a spartan apartment above the Green Gator. Their conversation was stilted and sterile.

Alex didn't think the car was the place to tackle *Drinking* or *The War* or *The Future* or, God forbid, *The Woman*, so he limited his questions to easy subjects. Jake limited his answers to monosyllables.

"Talked to your dad lately?" Alex asked. He hadn't seen Uncle Eddie in a few months.

"Nope."

"The bar doing a good business?"

"Yeah."

"You working there full-time?"

"I am."

"Heard you have a new girlfriend."

Finally, a reaction. Jake shifted his stare from the passing scenery to Alex. "Who told you that?"

"My mom, who doesn't think she's good enough for you,

which means she probably got it straight from your mom."

A half-smile. "Mom and Aunt Norma, the Titans of Picayune."

"So what's her name?"

"Madalyn." Jake crossed his arms, reclined his head on the headrest and closed his eyes. End of subject.

Alex dropped his cousin off in front of the Gator and went on the prowl for a parking spot off Bourbon Street—no simple task, even in the dregs of summer.

When he got back from carrying his overnighter four blocks, his shirt was soaked with sweat from the stifling humidity. Jake sat behind the bar at the near end of the long, narrow room. He wore a pair of dark-rimmed glasses and worked in a ledger, frowning in concentration.

Alex paused in the door as his eyes adjusted from bright sunlight to barroom darkness, watching his cousin make quick notations and calculations. Jake was a smart man, especially with numbers. He hadn't gotten his business degree on his looks.

According to Ken, whom Alex had called during the parking-spot hunt, Jake had been running the bar singlehandedly and turning a bigger profit in the last six months than they'd ever seen. He'd developed new marketing ideas and put together a proposal for a kitchen. Before this little stunt, Ken had hoped to sell his share of the business to Jake outright if Jake could get the financing. But selling a bar to a man with a history of alcohol problems and poor self-control could be like setting a terrier in a box full of rats.

There was always a chance the rats might win and, regardless, the fight would always be ugly.

Jake glanced up and pointed Alex to the barstool in front of him. "You look like a man in need of a drink."

"Abita." Alex took a sniff of Jake's Coke bottle while his cousin fetched the beer. No alcohol.

"It's straight," Jake said, sliding back onto his stool as he set the beer in front of Alex. "Might as well get it over with, whatever you got to say. I don't want to sit around watching you work up your nerve for a lecture while you drink my inventory."

Alex took a sip and watched as Jake answered a question for the bartender, a dark-haired beauty with café-au-lait skin. She'd already tossed a couple of smiles his way. Alex wouldn't mind getting to know her now that Cindy was firmly in the *ex* category.

Jake busted him mid-ogle. "Eyes front, mister. Leyla's off-limits. Now say what you've got to say."

Alex blew out a frustrated breath. He hated to yell at Jake when he looked so whipped.

Then again, Alex had given up his long weekend for this. "Fine." He set his bottle down with a thump. "What the *hell* are you doing, Jake? Two DUIs? You'll be lucky if they don't jerk your license, which they will if you get one more. You're gonna end up back in Picayune working at the family hardware store and getting—"

Jake had stopped listening. The arrogant son of a bitch wasn't even looking at him anymore. His eyes had focused on something past Alex's shoulder, something that had put a smile on his face.

Alex spun his stool around to see what—o r who—was so damned important. Definitely a *who*. She had her back to them, talking to some tourist types at a table. The woman was tall and slender, auburn-haired, wearing a black lacy thing up top and tight jeans that molded to her ass. And it was a mighty fine ass.

Alex shook his head to restart his brain in time for the woman to turn and steal his breath again.

She was perfect, and Alex wanted her, even as the gaze from her wide green eyes swept past him and locked on Jake. She moved with a grace that made Alex want to grovel and beg for her to look at him. He wanted to hit Jake and take her for himself.

Madalyn—because this had to be her—walked around the bar and pulled Jake toward her for a long, slow kiss. Alex watched, shifty-eyed, and his pants developed a buzzing tingle.

The tingle intensified to a jarring vibration, and he clamped his hand on his pocket in annoyance. The Tracker was going off. Damned wizards had the absolute worst sense of timing.

Jake and the redhead hadn't come up for air, so Alex swiveled away from them reluctantly and pulled the Tracker from his pocket. If it had gone from buzz to vibrate, it meant something preternatural was close.

A red dot pulsed in the center of the tiny screen, its steady rhythm speeding as he pivoted slowly on his stool. When it was pointed back at Jake and Madalyn, it went solid red.

Well, shit. The goddess of a woman sucking Jake's lips off his face might be sexy as hell, but she sure wasn't human.

Four

ALEX STUCK HIS CELL phone back in his pocket and thrummed his fingers on the table of the corner booth he'd taken at the Gator. Jake and the woman—er, *thing* — hadn't noticed his absence, and the call to the Elders hadn't helped.

His restless hands twitched at the scrap of napkin on the table, where he'd scribbled the names of the sentinels for the New Orleans region. It was really their job to rid the city of whatever flavor of preternatural Madalyn happened to be; enforcers were the last resort. But he hated to get Jake messed up with wizards. Alex had never met Gerald St. Simon, the New Orleans sentinel, or his deputy, Drusilla Jaco, but he'd bet a month's paycheck they were as prickly as every other wizard he'd met.

He folded the napkin and stuck it in his pocket. The Elders would keep the sentinels out of it unless he called.

Alex leaned back and sipped his beer, watching Jake and Madalyn and thinking about the reaction he'd had to her. From a distance, he could see she was pretty, but not kill-your-cousin pretty. Jake was no match for her. Alex couldn't see Madalyn's face, but Jake's eyes followed her every movement. Reminded him of the old dog their granddad used to have. Spike would sit at his and Jake's feet when they were kids, watching whoever was eating. They'd hold the food up and wave it around in the air, laughing as Spike's gaze followed their hands in whirligigs and circles.

That's how Jake watched Madalyn, like he was hungry for whatever scrap she might toss him. She had to be a prete that could enthrall. Alex ticked through the most likely culprits. It was daylight, so she wasn't vampire. Sirens showed up in New Orleans on occasion, but Madalyn had gotten in his head without singing a note. He'd place odds on nymph or demon. A nymph would wear Jake out and move on. A succubus would wear Jake out till she siphoned the life out of him— then she'd move on. Either way, some fool must have summoned her, and she'd obviously escaped.

The sexy bartender Leyla managed to get Jake's attention away from Madalyn briefly. The she-thing spun on the barstool to canvass the room. Her gaze roamed past Alex, then snapped back.

Alex felt her will beating against his mental barricades and gave her a slow smile. Her lips puffed out in a pouty frown, and a small wrinkle appeared between perfect brows. Enforcer Training 101: the mental shield. He was good at it.

Tipping down the rest of his beer, Alex slid from the booth and unfolded all six-three of height and two-forty of muscle, stretching a little for effect and chuckling as her eyes grew hooded. He knew what to do. Hell, it might even be fun.

He maintained eye contact as he approached, and Madalyn bit her bottom lip. Again, Alex felt her will looking for a way into his head. She was strong, and he had to concentrate—give her just enough eye contact so she'd think he was hooked but not enough to get hooked. At the last second, he veered to the bar and looked away from her altogether. The jukebox was between songs, so her low growl was audible.

He looked over his shoulder at his cousin. "Yo, Jake. The other upstairs apartment still empty?"

Jake glanced up from a stack of papers and handed them to the bartender. "Tell the distributors to hold off till tomorrow," he told her before turning back to Alex. "Yeah, it's unlocked— key's on the kitchen table. You staying?"

A tingle traveled across Alex's chest and straight to his groin when Madalyn put a hand on his shoulder. "Yeah." He had to choke out the word.

"Jacob, you haven't introduced us." Madalyn's voice was husky, her accent exotic.

"He's nobody you need to know." Jake glared at Alex. "Don't you have somewhere to be?"

Alex eased away from Madalyn's hand; he definitely didn't need to be touching her. "Yeah, I'm going up to my room." He retrieved his overnighter from behind the bar. "Gonna relax a while." He looked back at her. "Maybe get out of these clothes."

Her pupils expanded, then elongated and narrowed like a goat's. Succubus. He felt her gaze tracking him all the way through the bar, into the back hallway, and around the corner into the stairwell. It felt like spiders crawling under his skin.

Five

THE SPARE APARTMENT ON the second floor of the Green Gator had been decorated in the same crap as Jake's place across the small landing: early garage sale. Plaid sofa, brown naugahyde recliner with stuffing hanging out in tufts, scarred dining table with two rickety chairs constructed of something approximating wood. Alex had only stayed here once or twice—most of the Elders' business in New Orleans was handled by the sentinels, which was fine with him.

He loved the jazz and the big live oaks and the lacy iron balconies but along with all that came the dirt, the noise, the crime, and the infuriatingly inefficient and eccentric assortment of residents.

Alex pulled off the jacket, unstrapped the shoulder holster, and dug in the overnighter for his emergency supply of ammo; he had a partial clip of specially designed hollow bullets filled with holy water that had "demon" written all over them. Too bad the rest of his supply was still in the car. He popped in the clip and laid the pistol on the sofa next to him. Leaned back and waited.

Jake must have been holding on tight because it took her almost five minutes to arrive.

She walked in without knocking. Her green eyes were too bright, her hair too vividly auburn—some kind of glamour.

Alex rose slowly, letting her get an eyeful. Her naked, hungry gaze brought goose bumps to his skin as it washed over him, and the first prickles of doubt followed. In his desire to keep Jake separate from a world he didn't know about, Alex had broken the cardinal rule for any agent, whether FBI or enforcer: always go in with backup.

Too late, he realized he should've called the damned sentinels.

Madalyn came to stand in front of him and placed her palm on his chest, looking up at him suspiciously. "What are you, Alexander Warin?"

Had Jake told her his name, or was she that powerful? Her energy spiraled across his chest and he fought to keep her out of his head. Another mistake: he'd downed that beer.

Alex channeled his inner John Wayne. "I'm the man you never wanted to meet. It's time for you to go. Just fade back into the Beyond, or hell, or wherever you came from— no need for this to get messy." He grasped her wrist with his left hand in case he needed to grab the gun with his right, and kept his voice low. "But I don't mind making a mess."

She jerked her arm away and circled him. "You are not a wizard. I would be able to feel your power." She came to a stop in front of him, and cocked her head. "You are an enforcer, yes? You work for the wizards. What else are you?"

He raised an eyebrow but didn't answer. She didn't need to know he was a shapeshifter. Never volunteer information.

She smiled slowly, and he kept his eyes firmly on her nose—now that she knew what he was, she'd try harder to enthrall him. "You were foolish to meet me alone, Alexander. You are arrogant, and that is your weakness." She moved closer, until her too-perfect breasts brushed his chest. "Jacob will not live another week. I have enjoyed using him up at my leisure, but maybe I will finish him now that you have come to play. You will be more of a challenge. He was already damaged."

If Alex had needed proof that the succubus was behind Jake's recent downslide, now he had it. "Leave Jake," he said, taking a step backward. "I'm a better match for you." He lowered his voice. "But I need to know who I'm dealing with. What kind of demon name is Madalyn?"

She laughed, and for an instant the glamour dropped and the monster behind the pretty façade emerged. Lumpy, mottled skin of greenish-gray, dingy teeth that looked as if they'd been filed into points, hair the color of red licorice. Startled, Alex looked into her yellow, goat-slitted eyes—and couldn't look away.

The glamour washed back across her face but she changed her body, elongating it until she could look him in the eye.

Alex panicked and tried to move, but his limbs were no longer taking orders from his brain. Even his tongue wouldn't budge.

"Take off your shirt," Madalyn—or the thing that called itself Madalyn—ordered, and Alex fought it. He really did. He willed his hands to stop as they lifted to clutch the neck of his t-shirt. Ordered them to be still as they wrenched the shirt over his head and dropped it to the floor. Begged them to stay in place as they reached for her.

Madalyn laughed, a feral sound that shouldn't be heard outside a bedroom, and Alex's body responded to it. Lust threatened to wipe out reason, but the shock of her reaching around him and picking up the Colt was like a splash of ice water.

He'd forgotten the gun. What kind of enforcer forgot his weapon? He deserved to be shot with his own bullets full of holy water.

"You must not be very smart, Alexander," Madalyn said, echoing his own thoughts as she waved the gun by its barrel. The safety was off and with any luck, she'd shoot herself. But today hadn't been lucky so far.

"Put your arms around me." Madalyn poked him in the abs with the gun handle.

Please fire it. Shoot yourself, bitch.

But the gun didn't fire, and he mentally cursed his arms as they reached around her, stroking skin he shouldn't want to touch, eager for her to literally love him to death.

She stretched out an arm and dropped the gun on the coffee table with a clatter. He couldn't will his hands to leave her long enough to retrieve it.

Damn it, she'd kill Jake as soon as she finished with him, then find her next victim. He'd screwed up, big-time.

Six

ALEX DIDN'T HEAR JAKE come in, wasn't sure how long he'd been there watching what he thought was his girlfriend suddenly growing a foot taller and sucking out his cousin's soul—or whatever the hell he might think she was doing. Alex had become a bundle of nerve endings and constricting lungs, a pounding heartbeat and a growing whoosh of blood behind his eyeballs.

Jake appeared next to them, holding the Colt. Alex tried to remember if it was his gun, and why Jake would have it, or if his cousin had carried a Colt in the Marines. The sound of a handgun's clip being checked helped clear his head, and it finally attracted Madalyn's attention. She stepped back.

With her touch gone and eye contact broken, the effect on Alex was immediate. He could breathe again, and felt his brain re-engage like some rusty cog had slid into place and begun a halting rotation. When his rubbery legs gave way, he sat hard on the sofa.

Jake had the pistol pointed halfway between Madalyn and

Alex. "Don't come near me," he told her. "I haven't decided which one of you I'm gonna shoot first." Jake's voice was hard and his Mississippi drawl exaggerated. It was his macho, don't-mess-with-me voice. Alex had heard it a million times, although never with a gun behind it. His gun. He remembered that now.

"Jacob, look at me." Madalyn got Jake's attention, then dropped her glamour.

His face drained of color and he shifted the gun toward her. Alex didn't think he was making eye contact, though. "Holy hell. What are you?"

Alex was still struggling to his feet when Jake fired, and true to his cousin's training, the bullet hit home. Right in Madalyn's heart, or whatever demons had.

Alex had to move fast, needed to gain control. He fell back on habit, propelling himself off the sofa and straight into Jake. His head butted Jake's stomach with enough force to send them both sprawling.

The Colt flew against the lamp with a crash, and Jake was so rattled that Alex managed to get off three good punches—the last one an uppercut that caught Jake on the nerve just below the chin. Jake's head hit the wooden floor with a thump, and his eyes fluttered closed. Unconscious. Just the way Alex wanted him.

Alex rolled off him and looked at Madalyn, or what was left of her—a puddle of ectoplasm. Once her physical container was destroyed by the holy bullet, her rotted soul, or whatever made up her demonic essence, faded back into the Beyond. She'd live to be summoned another day. Hopefully far from here.

He retrieved the Colt from the floor, along with his t-shirt, and laid the former on the kitchen table with the holster. He pulled the latter over his head, settled into the recliner, and waited for Jake to wake up.

Must have been a damned fine uppercut, because it took his cousin a good fifteen minutes to fully come around. He finally sat up, rubbing his chin and jaw. A bruise already bloomed in the approximate shape of Alex's fist, and a trail of blood dripped off his lower lip. He blinked at Alex, then glanced around the room. "Where's Madalyn?"

So far, so good. Jake didn't seem to remember seeing the demon without its glamour.

"Gone," Alex said. "She called us a couple of rednecks and left us to fight it out."

Jake frowned, looked at his hands, held his right hand to his nose. "Only problem with that story, cowboy, is that these knuckles didn't hit anybody, you don't have a mark on you, and my hand smells like I fired a gun." He continued to stare at his hands, and his eyes widened.

Shit. He was remembering. Alex held his breath. If Jake remembered enough, Alex would have to call the sentinels after all, to alter his memories.

"You were fooling around with my pistol, talking bullshit, and it went off—nobody got hurt." Alex jerked his head toward the table.

Jake stared at the gun a moment, shook his head, and clambered to his feet. "Man, I gotta cut back on the whiskey. I had the craziest dream while I was out." He flopped on the end of the sofa nearest Alex's chair.

"Sorry I hit you so hard."

Jake flexed his jaw from side to side and wiped the blood from his chin with his shirttail. "That makes two of us. My brain feels like it's been shaken and stirred." He closed his eyes and leaned his head against the back sofa cushion. "Seems like I should be upset that Madalyn's gone, but truth be told, I'm kinda relieved. That woman was some kind of intense. I'm tired as hell."

Alex nodded. Jake had no idea.

They sat in companionable silence another few minutes before Jake hauled himself off the sofa. "Oh well. Headache or not, I need to get back downstairs. Leyla's a great bartender but she's not used to running things by herself."

Alex followed him to the door. "I'll just hang here tonight and head back to Jackson tomorrow. You gonna be okay?"

Jake turned to face him. "Be fine as long as I take care of one last thing."

"What?"

Alex didn't see the fist till a split-second before its impact with his bottom lip.

"That," Jake said, "was for kissing my girl. You're still

wearing her lipstick, shit-for-brains."

Alex grinned as he climbed to his feet and spat out a mouthful of blood.

Seven

JAKE WAS STILL SACKED out when Alex left the next morning. He pulled the apartment door shut behind him, stuck a note on Jake's door across the landing, and walked through the quiet, dark bar to let himself out the back. Every table had been cleaned, every ashtray emptied, the floors mopped. Even the bathrooms had their doors propped open and were as clean as any bar in the French Quarter that only closed between four and ten a.m. Jake knew how to run this place.

Alex strolled back to his car by a circuitous route so he could pick up a bag of beignets from Café du Monde. He stopped to sit on the benches in front of St. Louis Cathedral, eating and tossing occasional crumbs to the pigeons. The fortune-tellers and artists hadn't yet set up around Jackson Square, and the mule-drawn carts were lined up along Decatur Street, awaiting the hordes of bleary-eyed tourists that would soon be stirring. The air had a touch of coolness, and Alex could almost imagine he liked this place, saw the charm of it, understood why Jake had settled here and felt at home.

He pulled out his cell phone and called Ken Hachette.

"How much were you gonna ask Jake to buy you out of the bar?" he asked after giving Ken a highly censored account of Madalyn's exit and Jake's expected return to normal.

"Just what I put in when we bought it. He's done all the work to increase its value," Ken said. "You want to buy me out instead?"

Alex winced at the idea trying to share ownership of anything with Jake. "No, Jake's going to buy it; he just doesn't know it. I'll send you a cashier's check when I get home, but Jake can't know about it. That's the deal. Tell him you're handing it over gratis because you don't have time for it—or make something up he'll believe."

He paused. "And I don't care if you are a homicide detective. If you ever tell Jake the truth, I'll hunt you down."

He wasn't joking.

Ken remained silent for a few moments. "You sure you don't want him to know? It's a big thing you're doing."

Jake would never take help from him. Neither of them would ever admit it out loud, but they were more like brothers than cousins. Jake needed a break. Plus, Alex made a lot of money, way more than his family realized. The wizards considered his job extremely high-risk.

Imagine that.

"Consider it my good deed for the week," he told Ken. "We got a deal?"

Ken laughed. "You just bought yourself a half-share in a

good man's life, even if he won't ever know it."

Alex got Ken's address, ended the call, and watched the pigeons fighting each other for the last crumbs of beignet. As long-term investments went, it wasn't a bad one.

PIRATESHIP DOWN

Pirateship Down *is an all-new novella featuring wizard sentinel Drusilla "DJ" Jaco; her friend Rene Delachaise, a merman who mainstreams in the commercial fishing industry in Louisiana; and 19th-century French pirate Jean Lafitte, leader of the historical undead. Although it has a brief scene in New Orleans' Lakeview community and in Old Barataria in the Beyond, the bulk of the story takes place in modern Terrebonne Parish, Louisiana, including the community of Cocodrie and the city of Houma. There might be a jail and a prison jumpsuit involved. The events of* Pirateship Down *take place between* Elysian Fields *and* Pirate's Alley.

One

I WAS STILL A few dozen yards from the house, limping along the dark beach, when the sound of raised male voices reached me over the gentle waves wafting from the Gulf of Mexico.

"The wizard'll kill you if you do this. DJ's just hurt; she ain't dead." That was definitely the voice of the merman Rene Delachaise. Nobody could speak South Louisiana Cajun like my friend Rene, since that's exactly what he was. Well, the aquatic shapeshifter version of a Cajun.

"*Mon Dieu.* We shall return to the bosom of our homes before the lovely Drusilla even realizes we have departed. She is much too concerned with her dog." That French-accented baritone could belong only to the undead pirate Jean Lafitte, appropriate since the voices wafted from the open window of his study.

Awesome. I'd arrived in the Beyond unannounced to check on Jean's health, staggering down a mile of dark beach with an armload of andouille and brandy, only to hear the formation of some nefarious plot. Besides, my dog—Jean's not-so-affectionate reference to my boyfriend, Alex—was out of town, so I wasn't busy at all. I couldn't sleep and had a fierce, constant craving for chocolate.

In other words, I needed something to keep me from dwelling on the loss and pain that had been heaped around my life the last couple of months. What better way than to check on an ailing, immortal pirate?

When I'd stepped into the transport behind St. Louis Cathedral in modern New Orleans, it had been ten o'clock on a bright December morning. Within a brief compression of space and time, the transport had dumped me into the pitch dark of the remote open transport on Grand Terre Island, circa 1814—the otherworldly home of Jean Lafitte when he wasn't creating havoc in the modern world. The sun never shone in this corner of the Beyond.

Whatever Jean and Rene were arguing about, they didn't want me to know, which constituted grounds for eavesdropping. We'd all been through hell the last two months, physically and emotionally, with the preternatural world converging on New Orleans for what looked like an eventual power showdown. Now was not the time for half-baked piratical plots. I didn't have the heart for it.

Settling the sausage and brandy on the edge of the banquette stretching from the beach to the front door of Jean's tropical Grand Terre mansion, I sneaked onto the verandah next to the floor-to-ceiling window.

"You ain't in no shape to be searching for anything." Rene's voice rose and fell; he was pacing. "You just got killed again, or did you forget about that?"

"*Non*, Rene. A man does not forget his own death, even if it is not his first."

The historical undead were famous people granted immortality by the magic of human memory and, in New Orleans, early 19th-century privateer Jean Lafitte would never be forgotten. His legend had made him virtual royalty, a smuggling, seafaring French version of Robin Hood. Jean could be killed, but only temporarily.

His last death had occurred, at my reluctant hand, only two weeks earlier. Thus, the visit and the peace offerings.

"That ain't the point, pirate." I startled as Rene banged on something for emphasis. "You're gonna get yourself killed again, and either me or DJ will get killed tryin' to save you. We ain't immortal. If we get killed, we ain't comin' back. Stop being an entitled jackass."

Jean's voice rose loud enough to wake the undead. "You forget to whom you speak, Monsieur Delachaise, *vous laid gros poisson.*"

Holy crap. Rene had called Jean a jackass and Jean had called Rene a big, ugly fish. Time to intervene before they got in a fistfight, although it might be interesting. Jean was physically bigger, but Rene had absolutely no sense of self-preservation when it came to food, sex, or fisticuffs. We'd once shared a brain for twenty-four excruciating hours, so I knew this for a fact.

I leaned over to pick up the andouille and brandy, setting

off a waltz of pain between my bruised ribs and the half-healed gunshot wound in my shoulder. A groan escaped before I could stop it.

When I straightened up, both the pirate and the merman were charging toward the window.

"What you doin' here, babe?"

"You should be resting your delicate constitution, Drusilla. In the comfort of your own home."

Rene stepped onto the porch through the window and took the andouille, and Jean wrested the two bottles of brandy from my hands. Their spat had been forgotten, or at least abandoned for the moment.

"You must sit in the reclining chair, *Jolie*." Jean gestured like a game show host, showing off an addition to the early 19th-century furnishings in his study: an overstuffed leather recliner. It fit in like a priest at a bordello.

I sank into its pillowy comfort and allowed Jean to demonstrate the raising and lowering of the footrest as if I'd never before seen such a wondrous thing.

Rene, meanwhile, played host and poured us all generous glasses of brandy that flickered in the lamplight like amber jewels. My shoulder wound was mending quickly thanks to my own healing potion, but the wizard doctor had plied me with painkillers for the ribs. I wasn't sure how they'd mix with brandy. Then again, since I'd been having trouble sleeping, maybe it was worth a try.

Jean settled his large frame next to the shorter, wirier

Rene. They filled up the delicate white-upholstered settee, looking at me in expectant silence. I couldn't help but imagine them as dogs, waiting for commands to sit and fetch. Except I knew both would be more likely to bite than follow orders.

"What were you guys arguing about when I got here?"

They exchanged quick glances. Jean knew many things about me; my empathic abilities were not among them. Rene had a wonky shapeshifter energy that was hard for me to decipher, but Jean's feelings had the clarity of a large-print library edition of *Pirate Emotions*. His adrenaline spiked, which confirmed his preparation to evade the truth. *Lie* was such a harsh word.

"You were mistaken, *Jolie*," he said. "We were not arguing but merely enjoying a spirited discussion, which is of no matter now. Share with me how your injuries are healing, *s'il vous plaît*. I have been most concerned for your welfare."

Uh-huh. Fine. I'd play along for a few minutes. "I'm healing quickly but not sleeping much." Betrayal and attempted murder would do that to you. "You look well."

Of course, the pirate always looked extremely well. He was tall, dark-haired, and dangerous, not to mention the ripped physique and sexy accent. Through a colossal mess of betrayal and backstabbing preternatural politics, however, Jean had sacrificed his life to save mine last month. That act had changed the tenor of our relationship from mild flirtation to... something deeper. I hadn't yet figured out what that something might be.

"I am fully healed, *merci*," he said. "It is as if I were never wounded."

"Liar." Rene leaned over and gave Jean a hearty shoulder bump. The pirate's dark blue eyes winced.

No, he hadn't healed in the least. Which made whatever scheme he'd devised an even worse idea.

"Now, back to the important part. What are you two cooking up?"

Jean frowned a moment, then turned to Rene. "She is hungry, perhaps, and wishes for us to cook? You could prepare some étoufée."

"She ain't talking' about that kind of cooking, and you know it. Your English ain't nearly as bad as you like to pretend." Rene shook his head. "She's not gonna give up, pirate, so you might as well start talking."

"Bah." Jean crossed his arms, wincing again. "I have no words to say."

Well, there was a first. I'd never get a straight answer from the pirate, so I speared Rene with my best glare. "Rene? What's he up to?"

"I ain't telling you a thing, babe." Rene crossed his arms, mimicking Jean's posture.

Oh, good Lord. Rene would never lie to me, but that didn't mean he'd tell anything he didn't want me to know. Jean, on the other hand, had no qualms about lying.

I lowered the footrest on the recliner, stood up, and waited a few moments for the pain in my ribs to subside. It was awfully inconvenient to be a wizard who could do nifty elven fire magic and yet have nothing to combat internal injuries.

"Where are you going, Drusilla?" Was it my imagination, or did Jean sound a bit suspicious?

"I'm going to walk around your study for a few minutes. It makes my ribs hurt less than when I'm sitting."

Liar, liar, pirate on fire. I was ferreting for clues.

Jean's ornate wooden desk was immaculate but for a couple of rolled-up maps and a copy of this morning's *Times-Picayune*. I hadn't seen the paper in a few days, but the headline at the top of the fold answered all my questions in five short words:

SUNKEN LAFITTE TREASURE SHIP FOUND

Damn it. I snatched up the newspaper and began reading.

Early on Wednesday, an oil company's exploratory crew chanced upon a sunken vessel on the floor of the Gulf of Mexico just south of Terrebonne Parish. Scientists from the LSU marine archaeology program theorized that the schooner likely had been uncovered and washed from deep water toward the coast thanks to a recent storm. Carrying the name *Le Diligent*, the ship is believed to be the relatively intact remains of a vessel lost at sea during a storm about 1814 by men sailing under the flag of privateer and smuggler Jean Lafitte.

I looked up at Jean and Rene, who'd been watching me read. Rene wore a grin, and Jean did not. In fact, he looked annoyed.

"You"—I pointed my finger at the pirate as I limped back to the recliner—"are not going after that ship. You just got elected to represent the historical undead on the Interspecies Council, and this is exactly the kind of thing that will get you tossed off before they even hold their first meeting. Plus, you're injured."

And so was I. As sentinel of the New Orleans region, it was my job to keep preternatural citizens in line, not chase after them while they attempted nautical larceny.

Jean gave me his most charming smile, but it faded when he realized he was wasting his time. "I shall claim what is mine," he said, pointing a finger right back at me. "And there is nothing, Drusilla, that you might do to prevent this."

Two

JEAN HAD BEEN RIGHT: there was nothing I could do to prevent the inevitable. He was going after that ship, with or without my assistance.

"You know what they say, whoever *they* are." Rene walked with me from one unfinished room to another on the first floor of my house, also known as The Work in Progress. After my real house had been burned down by an undead serial killer last month, Alex had surprised me at Thanksgiving by making my father's former house semi-habitable. It had been stripped down to the studs after Hurricane Katrina.

"No, what do they say?" I hated *them*, whoever they were.

"If you can't beat 'em, join 'em so you can keep 'em out of hot water."

I thought Rene had played a little fast and loose with his interpretation of that particular cliché, but if the shrimp boot fit, might as well wear it.

"What do you think we might need?" It had taken Jean and Rene less than two hours to wear me down. Once I was convinced Jean couldn't be talked out of his harebrained scheme, my choices were limited. I either had to restrain him or help him.

The only bondage that interested me involved Alex Warin and a set of handcuffs, so I had to help Jean retrieve his boat or, more likely, prove that whatever he'd stashed on it two centuries ago couldn't be salvaged.

Plus, once I'd had time to think about it, a few days away from New Orleans might do us all good. Both Rene and I had lost people we loved in the last few months, and Jean had been betrayed by a man he'd considered a friend for more than two centuries. A change of scenery might not mend our hearts but it could at least provide a distraction—as long as we could stay out of trouble. None of us had proven very adept in that particular area.

Opening one of the plastic containers that currently served as a kitchen cabinet, I scanned the meager contents of my magical stash. The house had a functioning stove, but no Internet connection, which meant I could cook up potions but hadn't been able to buy supplies from the wizarding Elders' online supply house.

"How 'bout something to make us invisible?" Rene peered over my shoulder into the box. "You ain't got much magic stuff in there, DJ."

"Tell me about it." I studied the few common items I'd been able to pick up in the local grocery and health-food stores. "I can do a camouflage potion, and a few charms."

True invisibility wasn't possible, but I had a feeling magical camo might come in handy.

When I'd left Barataria yesterday, Jean and Rene had been arguing about the best way to get to Terrebonne Parish. Since Rene had shown up at my house in his truck, I assumed he'd agreed to drive.

"Did you volunteer to play chauffeur to Terrebonne Parish?" I poured a mixture of herbs and holy water into a glass bowl and employed my elven staff to ramp up the physical magical I used to infuse it. As a Green Congress wizard, I had plenty of ritual magic at my disposal. My physical magic needed all the ramping-up it could get.

Rene jumped up to sit on the counter. "It was the lesser of the evils. Jean had this crazy idea that you could create a big magical transport on the bottom of the Mississippi River bed, near Venice." That would be Venice, Louisiana, about ten miles from Rene's house.

"Then he decided I could sail my boat into the Beyond through that transport and pick him up in Old Barataria. Meanwhile, you'd drive to Terrebonne Parish, rent a boat, and create a giant transport in the Gulf of Mexico in time for him and me to sail through it into the modern world."

As if there were any doubt, he added, "I told him I ain't doin' that shit with my trawler."

I gaped at Rene. "I can't even swim. How the hell did he think I'd create a transport in open water by myself?"

"The pirate thinks you can do anything, babe." Rene grinned at me. "You sure got him fooled."

"Apparently." Lately, if I survived twenty-four hours without being shot or hacked at with an ax, I considered it a good day.

Rene leaned over to watch my concoction shoot puffs of condensation into the air above the bowl. "In fact, I told Jean I ain't gonna take out the *Dieu de la Mer* and risk her gettin' impounded, period. He don't have a clue how much a shrimp boat costs, not to mention the risk of losing my commercial fishing license."

I poured the completed camo potion into a pint-sized Mason jar, labeled it, and settled it into the oversized distressed-leather messenger bag I'd bought to replace the portable magic kit that had burned up with my house. "How long will it take us to get there?"

"It ain't that far," Rene said. "Two or three hours if the weather and traffic are good. We can rent a boat in Cocodrie— that's where the road stops."

The bottom third of Terrebonne Parish was mostly swamp.

I studied the contents of my box and mixed a couple of favorite charms I'd found useful in the past: confusion and sleep. Those, I put in small vials with caps that easily flipped off for quick throwing. Things could go south in a flash when Jean was involved.

Reaching inside the neck of my Tulane sweatshirt, I pulled out the magicked bag of herbs and stones I wore to minimize my empathic abilities and stashed it in the supply box. For this misadventure, I needed all the weapons in my arsenal, which meant the elven staff and my ability to read human emotions.

I tucked Charlie into the pack last and pulled my unruly blond hair into a ponytail. "Okay, I have a change of clothes, magic kit, some fake I.D.s, and my staff. I think that's it."

A real woman would embark on a weekend getaway with makeup and a swimsuit; I had charms and a variety of fake I.D.s. The discrepancy wasn't lost on me.

"You learned how to aim that thing any better, babe?" Rene poked at the staff, which threw off a couple of warning sparks. Charlie didn't like anyone else touching him. He was like a loyal pet, only made of wood and capable of shooting ropes of fire. "'Cause last time I checked, you couldn't hit anything smaller than a barn."

"That is simply not true," I said. "I hit my SUV gas tank. It was *much* smaller than a barn." Yes, I'd blown up my own vehicle.

"You weren't aiming at it, though," Rene pointed out.

We both looked up at the sound of footsteps overhead. The second floor of the house remained all flooring and studs, with none of the walls filled in yet. I did have a transport up there, however, and had given Jean the direct transport name: *Hogwarts*.

"Pirate's here." I grabbed my bag and tried not to groan at the tug on my shoulder. I didn't protest when Rene slid it off and set it beside the front door. He was the only one of the three of us without a physical injury.

When we reached the big, empty second floor, Jean was

leaning against one of the wall studs outside the transport. He looked pale in a stubborn, piratical kind of way.

"Jean, are you sure you want to do this now?" I reached up and put the back of my hand to his forehead. It felt warm, but who knew the normal body temperature of the historical undead? Could they even run a fever or get an infection? I had no idea. "We can do this after the Christmas holidays when we've both had time to heal. That ship isn't going anywhere."

"*Non*, I wish to procure my property before the government men claim it as their own."

I thought that ship had sailed, so to speak, but he wouldn't believe me. "Fine. Power through the pain then."

Jean shrugged. "Pain is but a fleeting matter, *Jolie*. One must not relinquish control to it, particularly when the ability to seek one's due reward is in peril of being lost."

Oh brother. Spare me from pirate philosophers. Whatever reward he sought probably was long gone, getting within a mile of the wreck site was doubtful, and I'd likely need magic to waylay any hovering government men. I'd gone through all those arguments yesterday to no avail.

"Okay, then, let's go." I looked around the room. "Where is your stuff?"

Jean smiled. "What does a man need, Drusilla, other than fresh sea air and the company of a beautiful woman?"

I gave him a level stare. My shoulder throbbed and I was in no mood for undead flirtation. "Toothpaste and underwear come to mind."

Rene made a rude noise. "Talk about panties in the truck. We need to get movin'."

Three

WE MADE IT TO the city of Houma before I was driven to violence. Once we'd finally gotten Jean off the topic of underwear, he'd proven curious about the world flying past the passenger-seat window of Rene's jacked-up black pickup.

He wanted to know about interstates and how they differed from other roads.

He asked about various types of vehicles and demanded to know why they had names like *Rogue* and *Renegade* but no one had a *Privateer*. He didn't ask about cars named *Pirate*, not being fond of the term.

He was fascinated by the 18-mile-long Atchafalaya Basin Bridge, and waxed philosophical on how long it took him to cross the massive swamp back in his human days.

He wanted to know how fast, exactly, Rene's truck would go. Thank God the merman refused to demonstrate.

The tunnel beneath the Gulf Intracoastal Waterway in Houma was almost our undoing.

"We are driving an automobile beneath the water?" Jean stuck his head out the open window and studied the tunnel roof zipping past us overhead. "I wish to pass through here once more, Rene. We must do this now. *Tout de suite*."

Grumbling, Rene indulged him, turning around and going through the tunnel the other way, then doing it all again.

"I wish to walk through it," Jean said. "This is a most wondrous thing. We must do this now."

"No." Rene kept driving through the semi-urban sprawl of Houma, the last town of any size before we entered the wilds of southern Terrebonne Parish, aka The End of the World As We Know It.

Frowning, Jean did his spoiled toddler impression and reached across me to grab the steering wheel.

"Get him off me, wizard. Make yourself useful." Rene slapped at Jean's hand and whapped me in the head instead.

I gave Jean a quick zap on the arm with Charlie, and he looked at me as if I'd killed his puppy. Jeez.

"Sorry, I shouldn't have done that," I said, mentally chastising myself. I should've just beaten him over the head with the staff. I didn't normally use my magic thoughtlessly, and the fact I'd zapped him in such a knee-jerk way reminded me how much healing I still had to do, mentally as well as physically. My nerves were raw.

Any lingering awkwardness was dispelled by Rene who, hearing a familiar set of drum riffs on the radio, turned it up full blast and began singing Taylor Swift's "Shake It Off" at the top of his off-key merman lungs. Jean and I looked at each other in mutual horror.

"Roll up the window before we get arrested for disturbing the peace!" I yelled at Jean over Rene's warbling about "haters gonna hate."

Rene effectively killed all conversation when the radio segued into "Bohemian Rhapsody" and he grew quiet, then quickly leaned forward and turned off the music. "That was one of Robert's favorite songs," he said. "I ain't ready to hear it."

Rene's twin brother had died a couple of months earlier, and this was the first time I'd heard him speak Robert's name. Jean and I weren't the only ones with healing to do. We drove on in silence, tunnels and Taylor Swift forgotten as we headed deep into the heart of rural Terrebonne Parish.

I'd lived in New Orleans most of my life. I'd taken day trips to most spots along the I-10 corridor between NOLA and the Texas state line, but I had to admit most of my knowledge of things south of Houma I knew only, collectively, as "the swamp."

The farther south we drove, the more foreign everything looked. It wasn't just the open, flat expanse of grasses like the marshes around Rene's swimming grounds in Plaquemines Parish. This was classic cypress swamp intersected by a very narrow road that led straight south to our destination, Cocodrie. The landscape was broken up occasionally by fields of sugar cane.

South of Cocodrie, one could only travel by boat, especially if one were in search of a sunken pirate ship.

We pulled into the community about forty-five minutes later. It was probably what most of Louisiana's second-largest parish would look like in another few decades. All the houses and fishing camps—weekend getaways for sport fishing, mostly—were raised on high piers to protect them from the frequent floods that immersed this low land outside the federal levee system. They lined up in rows on either side of the narrow roadway until the tarmac ran out.

Below Cocodrie lay hundreds of small, unconnected spits of land, dozens of bayous, the massive Terrebonne Bay, and then, finally, Isles Dernières—the last islands —and the Gulf of Mexico.

Rene pulled into a marina and we gathered the paperwork. Both Rene and I had driver's licenses, and Rene had brought his boating and fishing licenses from the state wildlife and fisheries department. Easy peasy.

Until he handed them to me. "Change my name," he said. "I ain't puttin' my real name on nothing. You know this ain't gonna go smooth."

Rene jerked his head toward the open passenger door of the truck, which Jean had vacated as soon as he smelled the sea air. "The pirate is pissed off about the way things stand with the Interspecies Council and what happened last month, plus he ain't healed yet. He's gonna cause problems."

I turned to look at Jean, who had assumed his best pirate stance—feet wide apart, arms crossed over his chest, gaze fixed on the horizon where it was hard to tell the sky from the water. He was in his element. All he needed was a freaking pirate ship.

"Yeah, you right." I sighed and dug in my messenger bag for a basic illusion charm, then spread the fine powder of magicked herbs over the top of both Rene's and my driver's licenses and his boating papers. "Who do you want to be?"

"Denis Villere," he said without hesitation. I grinned as I illusioned the name of his arch-enemy, who headed a rival merfolk clan, onto the documents. I also pulled out a fake photo identification card I'd prepared ahead for "Jean Breaux."

We needed one person with a legitimate credit card for deposits, and I agreed to be that person. If the human authorities ever came looking for me because of any chaos that transpired, I had spells and charms at my disposal. Being a wizard had its privileges.

An hour later, we had a two-bedroom cabin for the next three nights and the use of a 30-foot fishing boat that met with Rene's approval but looked as big as a house. Not to mention it cost a fortune. I made a mental note to start a tab for the pirate; I was by far the poorest person on this little outing.

"Couldn't we do with something smaller?" I watched Rene hook the boat trailer to the back of his truck.

"Babe, we're going in open water at least thirty miles offshore. Jean, he can swim good. You know I ain't gonna drown. Think of this boat as your life insurance policy."

Well, when he put it that way. "Does it have life jackets on board?" I eyed a black cloud building ominously on the southern horizon.

Rene ignored me. "We gonna stay here tonight and go out early in the morning. Me and Jean, we gotta look at the maps first and, anyway, there's a storm blowing in."

"*Oui*, one does not set sail late in the day." Jean joined us. "This is a time for making plans, for enjoying good wine, and for eating a fine meal prepared by the hands of a beautiful woman."

They both looked at me and I mimicked Jean's pirate stance.

"Yeah, well, we better find a restaurant then," Rene said, turning back toward the truck.

Four

I AWOKE EARLY THE next morning to an icy cold room, but I was warm and comfortable with my big, toasty shapeshifter curved around my back.

Then I awoke further and realized my big, toasty shapeshifter was in Picayune, Mississippi, visiting his parents.

Whoever had me all spooned up was too big to be my wiry merbuddy, which left only one option. I freed my left arm and shot my elbow back with all my strength. The arm tightened around my waist.

"Jean Lafitte, if you don't move that arm, I'll burn it off with the elven staff. Don't think I won't do it."

The pirate chuckled and rolled to his back. I peered around cautiously. I had slept in a pair of pajama pants and a Hansen's Sno-Bliz t-shirt, but I feared seeing more pirate than I was prepared for. He'd had the good sense to keep on his pants, although I shouldn't have been surprised. Jean had his own relaxed rules in terms of property procurement, but had turned out to be quite old-fashioned when it came to women. He wanted to win me over, not take me by force.

"You weren't here when I went to sleep." I'd have remembered. "Why are you here now?"

"Rene's snores sound much like an alligator claiming his territory. One does not find rest easily among such noise."

Yeah, well, he'd have to put up with it. Explaining to Alex that I'd helped Jean find his ship was one thing. Telling him I let the pirate sleep with me to avoid Rene's gatorlike snoring was not a conversation I planned to have.

I walked over to my bag and rifled around for my jeans and sweater. "I'm going to get dressed. When I return, I expect you to be somewhere else."

"Ah, *Jolie*. You have no sense of *l'amour*." With a put-upon sigh, Jean stood up and I looked at him in horror. His chest wound was a blackened mass over his breastbone, the skin spreading from it, red and angry.

"Oh, Jean." I wanted to cry, knowing I'd done that to him. "I'm so sorry."

"Do not fret, Drusilla." His voice was soft. "This was my choice. I will heal. Had I been forced to kill you, I would not heal from that and neither would you, *non*?"

"I'll make a healing potion for you when I get home. It will help." I should have done it already.

He grinned. "By that time, I shall have my ship again, *oui*?"

I seriously doubted it, but I'd play along. "*Oui*."

Twenty minutes later, dressed and with my hair still damp from the shower, I ventured outside and looked down from the front balcony. Below me, Rene and Jean leaned over the hood of the pickup, studying a large map.

Rene looked up when he heard my boots on the steps leading down from the cabin-on-stilts. "About time you finished your beauty routine, babe. We're burnin' daylight."

The sun was barely up, much less burning. "That shipwreck isn't going anywhere, and I want breakfast."

"I got jerky and cookies. We'll manage." Rene folded the map and dug his keys out of his pocket. "Let's get this done."

Note to self: Do not rely on a merman for breakfast. "What kind of cookies?"

He tossed a bag of alligator jerky in my lap when I climbed in the truck, followed closely by Jean.

"No way. Too much salt." I handed the jerky to Jean, who pulled out a strip and chewed it, studying the bag with interest.

"It's got lean protein. Besides, salt sure don't bother you when it's in pepperoni." Rene reached behind the seat and tossed a bag of Fig Newtons at my head. I caught them. Now we were talking.

I ate a dozen on the way to the marina, so I was on a sugar buzz by the time Rene backed the boat up to the choppy blue water. All kinds of trucks and boats crowded the launch, this being the height of redfish season, according to our resident merman and fisherman.

Fortified with plenty of sugar along with two capsules from the industrial-sized bottle of motion-sickness medicine in my bag, I climbed onto our rental boat. It was big, solid, and white, with *The Golden Girl* written in black script near the front of the hull.

"This name is a good omen that we shall find the treasure we seek, do you not agree?" Jean asked, climbing aboard behind me.

Either that or the boat was old and ready for a retirement home in South Florida, but I wouldn't share that bit of cultural trivia. "I'm sure it's an excellent omen."

Once Rene was aboard, I relaxed in a seat on the foredeck while the merman and the pirate fought over who got to drive the boat. I had slathered on sunscreen, put on my sunglasses, and prepared myself for a pleasant day on the water, at least until we got shot at or I felt the need to barf over the side of the portside rail, whichever came first.

"That pirate is outta control, babe." Rene flopped into the chair next to mine. They'd been set up for the comfort of anglers, but probably not the kind of angling we were up to. "Figured I might as well let him relive his glory days now, 'cause soon as we get close to where we think that research ship is, he ain't gonna be behind the wheel."

"Does he know how to drive this boat?" I figured navigational equipment had changed a bit in the past two centuries.

"Yeah, I've let him take the *Dieu de la Mer* out a little," Rene said. "He learns quick."

"You think he'll agree to let you take over once we get close?" Sounded out of pirate character to me.

"Hell no, but that's what you're here for," Rene said. "Pirate control."

Awesome. "And here I thought it was to keep you two from getting yourselves killed or arrested."

"That too."

I'd done a little online research on my tablet before turning in last night. A research vessel from LSU, *Geaux Tiger*, had taken the lead in preserving and exploring the site, and divers with cameras were making daily trips to catalog the ship. Until it could be studied in situ, and as long as no tropical storms came in to dislodge it, no one would attempt to move it.

What I hadn't read was the exact location of the wreckage.

"How do you guys know where to go?" I offered Rene my bottle of sunscreen and he gave me the look one might give a gibbering chimpanzee; guess mermen didn't have to worry about skin cancer. It was very rare among wizards, but with my propensity for chaos, I figured if it were possible to get it, I would.

"We're just gonna cruise in a pattern, hoping we spot that research ship. The guy that rented us the boat mentioned a particular place to avoid, so I figure that's where we need to go." Rene propped his feet on the rails. "Once we find them, we'll fish a while until they leave for the night. Then I'll do a dive."

Sounded nice and logical, but I had a prickly feeling at the back of my neck. Anything involving Jean could go bad quickly; it wasn't carelessness or lack of understanding. He was the smartest person I'd ever met. The pirate had his own soundtrack, however, and thought the rest of the world should march to it. Rene was an adrenaline junkie, but he at least understood things like the long-term ramifications of modern criminal activity.

By the time we spotted a small, tidy vessel with the LSU logo on the hull, it was well after lunchtime. I'd already eaten the rest of the Fig Newtons, more out of boredom than hunger.

Rene disappeared into the wheelhouse, and the metallic groan of the anchor sounded from beneath the deck. After a brief conversation with Jean, he walked to the aft deck, pulling his black t-shirt over his head. He had his jeans unzipped and had begun lowering them a couple of inches before my shocked brain registered why he was stripping like a Bourbon Street dancer on crack.

"Why are you gonna shift now?" I didn't want Rene to shift, not while the researchers were nearby. That left me alone on board with a pirate who'd been watching the other boat with way too much interest.

"If I see what they're photographing, it'll help me understand what kind of shape the wreckage is in and where valuable things might be." I averted my eyes as Rene finished his quick striptease. I'd never met a shifter with body issues, and I'd seen everything Rene had to offer—down to a particular tattoo of a bottle-nosed dolphin in a place that had to have hurt like hell. The man had more ink than a stationery shop.

"Keep an eye on the pirate." Rene walked to the back of the boat, out of sight of the research vessel, and nimbly slid atop the rail.

I finally looked at him, another horrific thought occurring to me. "What if you get a hook in your mouth or something?" Rene could shift partly into classic mer form, or could shift fully into a fresh- or saltwater dolphin, depending on which was needed. "You don't want to end up on a taxidermist's table."

Rene shot me a bird and flipped backward off *The Golden Girl*, leaving me alone with the pirate.

I swiveled around to make sure Jean was behaving himself, and he seemed content. He'd picked up the "double spyglass," as he called the binoculars, and was studying the *Geaux Tiger*. As for that vessel, I couldn't see much other than a few people in the wheelhouse. I assumed they had divers down at the wreckage. Hope they enjoyed their visit from an overly inquisitive dolphin.

"Hey, DJ!"

Rene's voice came from the front side of the boat, so I returned to the foredeck and leaned over the rail. He'd done a half shift; I could see the big silvery-blue dorsal fin wafting lazily under the water.

"What?"

"Make sure you don't let Jean raise anchor or move the boat—I'm using it to keep track of where I am." His voice sounded strained.

"What's wrong? Is visibility bad?"

He paused. "I don't like open water. It kinda freaks me out."

With that pronouncement and a big splash, he sank out of sight.

I pondered that revelation for a moment. Rene had fast become one of my best friends. How could I not know the merman was agoraphobic?

I glanced back at the wheelhouse and didn't see Jean. A quick look around the deck didn't reveal him, either, so he must have gone below into the small living area and kitchen.

Good. Maybe he'd take a nap, which is what I fully intended to do. I slathered on more sunscreen and resumed my spot on the foredeck, spreading Rene's abandoned map over my face.

The day was sunny but not humid, and a cool breeze added to the comfort. The gentle waves lulled me in and out of a doze, and I woke to an odd wisp of dream about the old TV show *Flipper,* whose reruns I used to watch as a kid.

Except when I opened my eyes and pulled the map off my face, Flipper continued his urgent, chirping noise.

Rene!

I raced to the side of the boat closest to the research vessel. The people—two men and a woman, I now saw—who'd been in *Geaux Tiger's* wheelhouse had gathered on their own deck.

I looked down, expecting to see Rene at the end of a hook or trapped in a net. Instead, he swam alongside a small rubber boat, chittering and bobbing his head as its big French oarsman propelled it toward the LSU vessel. I could practically decipher Rene's dolphin-speak. It contained a lot of f-words.

After a few shocked heartbeats, I found my own voice. "Jean, what the hell do you think you're doing?"

He yelled back without turning. "The time has come for me to claim what is mine, Drusilla."

Holy crap. Jean Lafitte was going all pirate on my ass.

Five

I DIDN'T KNOW WHAT to do. Jean had taken the lifeboat and I couldn't swim.

"Rene!" I shouted at the dolphin. Okay, I shrieked like a fishwife, not caring that some of the research vessel denizens had shifted their gazes toward me. Flipper did an impressive air dive, splashing Jean with a heavy spray of water before submerging to, I hope, shift back and help me figure out how to get the pirate off a collision course with disaster.

Jean shot a dirty look at the disappearing dorsal fin of his merman business partner, wiped water off his face, and finished his approach to the research vessel. At least maybe Rene could pull *The Golden Girl* alongside *Geaux Tiger* and we could retrieve Jean before he did anything that would require an army of Blue Congress wizards to fix. As a Green Congress wizard, I could mix a mean potion and cast an impressive array of spells and charms, but I couldn't create complicated illusions, shift time, or permanently modify memories like my Blue Congress counterparts.

Not to mention the fact that asking for a magical cleanup

team would get me in more hot water with the wizards than one could fit into the Gulf of Mexico.

By the time Rene stomped around the wheelhouse from the foredeck ladder, pulling on his pants and shaking water out of his hair, Jean had reached the research boat. One unsuspecting scientist had leaned over to help him aboard.

"DJ, why the hell you let him do that? You know what kind of shit he can stir up!" Rene leaned over the rail, cursing under his breath. Jean already had begun waving his hands in the air and running his mouth. At least so far, he hadn't pulled out a weapon.

"Take us over there." We needed to intervene before it was too late.

"What you gonna say?" Rene tugged on his Wild Tchoupitoulas t-shirt and his shoes. "Cause I can guarantee you he's already told 'em he's Jean Lafitte and he wants his ship back."

"Maybe not. Jean's short-tempered, but he's smart."

"Yeah, he's looking pretty smart right now." Rene strode toward the wheelhouse, leaving me to watch Jean and a short, bespectacled man with thinning hair and khaki pants engaged in what appeared to be a heated discussion. There was much pointing and hand-waving.

I'm a self-professed geek so I recognized one of my brethren. Jean's adversary was a bonafide, pocket-protector-wearing academic. The poor guy didn't stand a chance against a 230-year-old French pirate with a chip on his broad shoulders and a muzzle-loaded pistol hidden beneath his white linen tunic.

Beneath me, the deck vibrated as Rene hauled up the anchor and slowly turned *The Golden Girl* toward *Geaux Tiger*. The twain was about to meet and, in honor of the occasion, I stuffed a couple of confusion charms in the pocket of my jeans.

Two people aboard the *Tiger* broke off from the crowd watching The Jean Lafitte Show and approached the side as Rene stopped our boat within hopping-aboard range. "Okay if we come over there?" Rene asked. "My cousin"—he gestured in Jean's direction—"got away from us."

"You need to get him out of here." The male student grabbed the rope Rene tossed over the rail and secured the two boats together. Rene nimbly climbed over both sets of railings, then reached back to pull me aboard. Accent on *pull*. Halfway through my awkward stumble over the rail, a sickening crunch and a trail of thick liquid down my right thigh told me the confusion charms were goners. At least they were far enough from my face that I didn't have to worry about confusing myself.

The other student, a tall, rangy girl with a dark-brown ponytail, glanced at Jean. "Does he have, uh, mental issues?"

"He's batshit crazy," Rene said, turning to rest a squinty-eyed gaze on me. "Just ask her. This is his old lady."

My mouth dropped open, torn between indignation at being called old and Rene's implication that I was Jean's wife.

The young woman, who introduced herself as Amy something and was, indeed, a grad student in marine archaeology, grabbed my arm and steered me toward the foredeck. "Ma'am, Professor Patterson is threatening to call the Coast Guard. If you can get your husband off the boat, it'll just blow over."

The Coast Guard? Husband? I already had an unwanted elven bond-mate; I needed an undead French faux-spouse like New Orleans needed more praline shops. I needed any involvement with the U.S. Coast Guard even less, however.

I shot Rene a fish-kill look over my shoulder and marched toward where my significant pirate had grown cold and silent. That was a bad, bad sign. If Jean pontificated and made a spectacle of himself, he was mostly blowing hot air. When he grew quiet, things often took a dicey turn.

"I order you to leave this vessel immediately, Mr. Lafitte or whatever your name is." Professor Patterson's face turned an alarming shade of dark pink, which didn't look good with his purple and gold sweater vest and white turtleneck. Not that sweater vests looked good with much of anything.

Damn it. Jean hadn't even used the Jean Breaux alias on his fake I.D.

I slipped up behind him and tucked my left arm through his right, reaching down to twine the fingers of my hand firmly through his. It stopped those fingers' progress toward his hip, where I knew he had both his pistol and a triangular-bladed knife sheathed beneath his pirate tunic.

"Hi, honey." I bumped my shoulder against his, a ploy designed to unlatch his fierce gaze from the face of Dr. Patterson. "You're not causing problems for these nice people, are you?"

Jean looked down at me with cold eyes. "*Qu'est-ce que c'est* honey?"

He knew perfectly well what I meant, and I clenched my fingers more tightly as he tried to pull his hand from mine.

"I'm so sorry, professor." My empathic abilities were making a nasty cocktail of Jean's annoyance, the professor's relief, and my own shaky nerves. "My husband wasn't supposed to leave the boat. His cousin and I just checked him out of the home today for an outing."

Behind me, Rene coughed and, beside me, Jean looked confused. Which was a good expression for a man on a day-outing. "He's been absolutely fascinated with this whole story about finding Jean Lafitte's lost treasure ship," I said, pulling Jean farther from the professor and closer to Rene. "He's always been obsessed with our favorite privateer."

The professor laughed. His skin had lightened back to a sunburned pink. "I understand. Glad you'll be able to take him back to the, uh, *home*."

"I do not wish to go home. I wish to reclaim *Le Diligent*, which rightfully belongs to me, Jean Lafitte." Jean jerked his hand away with a violence that almost spun me off the side of the boat. "You will not deter me in this, *Jolie*. Nor you, Rene."

"My name's Denis," Rene reminded him. "And we need to

go for now. The men in white coats will be waiting for us. We'll bring you back to claim your ship later."

Patterson's roller-coaster emotions took another nosedive toward calm. He apparently trusted Rene's ability to control Jean more than mine. Smart man. I had no clue how to get him turned around and back on our boat without using Charlie. The elven staff was strapped to my calf inside my jeans, but it was a last resort. Fires and boats made bad companions for wizards who couldn't swim.

"There is actually something quite funny about this situation." Dr. Patterson nodded his encouragement as Rene tugged Jean toward the side rail closest to *The Golden Girl*. The mer might not be a big man, but Rene's shifter strength would allow him to toss the pirate to the other boat's deck with ease should that become necessary.

"Funny how?" I saw absolutely nothing humorous about this turn of events.

"One of my ancestors was Commodore Daniel Patterson—he wiped out a big chunk of Jean Lafitte's fleet and cleaned out his pirate den back in 1814 in Barataria." The professor shrugged, ignoring my frown and subtle head-shaking—he needed a big dose of shut-the-hell-up. "Of course, he wasn't able to keep the ships he captured but he kept all the pirate's money. It's a favorite family story."

Before I could warn Rene that he needed to hold Jean in a death grip, the merman tackled me to the deck. A split-second later, the world exploded with a deafening boom, and the acrid odor of burning gunpowder filled the air. I looked up at the sight of Jean, dark-cobalt eyes ablaze, aiming his bigass pistol straight at the professor. His shot had gone over the bow, taking the hearing from my left ear with it.

"If your tale is true, Monsieur Patterson"—Jean spit out the words as he reloaded his pistol—"then Jean Lafitte shall take your ship in return for the commodore's crimes, as well as the ship that lies below the water. I shall allot you five minutes for yourself and your crew to embark on the lifeboat, or else you will be forced over the rail. You might swim ashore, but I doubt it is within your ability to do so."

Jean glanced down at me as I struggled to my feet alongside Rene. "It is only due to the delicate sensibilities of Madame Lafitte that I spare your lives at all," he added.

Oh, give me a break. "Jean, put down that gun or we're getting a divorce and you're going to live in Old Barataria forever." I put as much force into my words as I could, but he was beyond hearing. I'd never seen him in such a stew.

I turned to Rene, who simply stood behind me with his arms crossed and a resigned expression on his face. "Do something," I hissed at him.

"Babe, we're screwed no matter how you slice that gator up," he said, jerking his head toward the rise of land barely visible to our north. "We got bigger problems."

The siren reached my ears before I saw the boat. Make that *boats*, plural. Two of them coming from different angles. One was shiny, white, and flew a U.S. flag off the back; the other was black with gold stripes, small, speedy, and already close enough for me to read the markings on the side: *TERREBONNE PARISH SHERIFF.*

Six

"BAH, THE GENDARMES." JEAN finished reloading his pistol and assessed the boats heading our way, sirens and lights on full blast. He turned to me, the picture of cold-blooded calm. "Do you have your magic stick or a pistol? We must fight."

My elven staff was the last thing I needed. One did not set sheriff's deputies or Coast Guard officers on fire. Or shoot them. Although shooting myself might not be a bad idea.

My confusion charms had soaked into the top of my shoes. Unless I took off my Nikes and began smacking people in the face with wet socks, that option was off the table.

"No, I do not have a weapon. And no, we must not fight." I reached up, grabbed a fistful of pirate shirt, and jerked Jean's head close enough for us to bump eyebrows. He only let me get away with it out of pure shock. "Listen, mister. This is not the time for acting like a big, French, entitled *privateer.*"

I lowered my voice and assumed a tone that brooked no argument. "You are going to be polite and humble with the *gendarmes.* You are likely going to be arrested, and you *will* allow them to put you in handcuffs or restraints." His brows formed one long, unhappy line across his face, so I talked faster. "You are going to tell them the truth—who you really are, except for the undead part, and what you want."

I figure in this case, truth was his best defense. They'd think he was delusional.

His gaze dropped, inappropriately, to my mouth. "And who am I to say you are, Drusilla? Are you a wizard or are the wife of Jean Lafitte?"

Oh good Lord, please let Alex never find out about this. "I am your wife, Jane Breaux." I could create an illusioned I.D. in that name, and it would ensure they let me visit him. I just hope he didn't know about the concept of conjugal visits.

I released his shirt and he straightened up with a small smile on his face. Also inappropriate, but being calm and horny when the cops arrived would reinforce his unstable mental status.

The Terrebonne Parish Sheriff's Office water patrol boat reached us first, and two officers approached the front of their vessel with a wary friendliness they'd no doubt developed to look unthreatening to miscreants.

"What's the problem here, folks?" The older of the officers, thirtysomething with a neat moustache, a bright yellow shirt, and a navy ballcap with SHERIFF printed in yellow across the front, gave us all an assessing look. "Is one of you Dr. Patterson?"

"That's me." The professor raised his hand as if in a classroom, anxious to earn a bonus grade by being a snitch.

"He"—a shaky finger pointed at Jean—"tried to shoot us. He was about to throw us overboard when you got here. He thinks he's Jean Lafitte."

"*Mon Dieu. Monsieur*, that—" Whatever outrageous thing Jean was about to say was cut short when I stomped on his foot, then kicked his ankle for good measure.

"Shut up," Rene hissed behind us.

"If we are to be wed, we must discuss your manners, Drusilla," Jean whispered. "They are most unsuitable."

Yeah, whatever.

"Do I have permission to board your vessel?" The deputy, whose shirt identified him as S. Leclerc, addressed his question to the professor but his hard gaze was squarely on Jean, Rene, and me. Awesome.

"Please." The professor waved the officer aboard. "Would it be all right for my students to wait below while we sort this out?"

"Afraid not." Deputy Leclerc was obviously not a trusting soul. "They can go on the aft deck with my partner, Officer Dumars, and if you have divers below, they'll need to join the rest of the students. He'll take their statements." Officer Dumars looked younger than the grad students, only better armed.

"Are there any firearms aboard the ship?" The deputy looked at Jean, who crossed his arms over his chest.

"Yes, sir. My husband has an antique pistol," I said in a bright, happy voice. "It accidentally went off. Jean, give your pistol to the deputy."

Jean ignored me.

"Better do it, pirate," Rene murmured. For some reason, he could call Jean a pirate without repercussions. "We'll get you out. Just let 'em have their way for now."

"Mon Dieu." Jean raised his tunic and reached for the pistol. Before he got halfway there, Deputy Leclerc and his partner both had big, black firearms aimed at him.

"Move slowly, sir. Place the weapon on the deck and kick it toward us."

I held my breath, waiting for a big French tantrum, but Jean behaved himself. He slowly removed the gun, held it out handle first, and placed it on the deck. Stretching out one long leg, he kicked the gun gently in the deputy's direction.

The pirate seemed to have done this before.

"Do you have any additional weapons, sir? Or your friends?"

Jean pulled his triangular dagger from its sheath and held it a moment before sending it, too, sliding across the deck. He'd considered throwing the damned thing. I know because I'd felt his brief surge of adrenaline. Now he'd settled back to cold anger.

"Anything else?"

"Non, Monsieur. Mais si je devais avoir un autre poignard, et je vous l'enverrais directement dans le cœur."

Leclerc narrowed his eyes. "You just added threatening a law enforcement officer to your list of charges, sir.

Comprendre?"

I should've warned Jean that he was more likely to encounter French-speaking citizens here than anywhere else in the state. Expressing the wish to throw a dagger straight into the heart of a deputy? Bad, bad idea.

"*Oui.*" Jean wore a suitably contrite expression, but his anger simmered.

I stepped forward, hands out. "Officer, cousin Rene and I brought my husband fishing today; he's had some emotional problems and frequently imagines himself to be Jean Lafitte. He's really harmless." A shuffle sounded behind me, probably Cousin Rene getting a death grip on Jean. "This is all a simple misunderstanding."

"He shot at us. That was no misunderstanding." Dr. Patterson puffed up like a blowfish with a Ph.D.

If Jean had truly shot at him, the man would be dead. I thought it best not to point that out, however. "He wanted to show off his antique pistol, seeing as how you were bragging about your ancestor knowing the real Jean Lafitte." I kept the snark in my voice to a minimum.

"He tried to murder us and throw us overboard," the professor said, assuming the smug, superior look one found only among members of the social elite and tenured faculty.

The young officer and the grad students, now joined by two divers, trooped to the aft deck, leaving Jean, Rene, and me alone with Dr. Patterson and Deputy Leclerc. We outnumbered them, but only for a few seconds. The U.S. Coast

Guard vessel had pulled alongside and two badasses jumped aboard. They wore identical navy shirts and pants, and were loaded down with big black guns that would give Alex Warin an orgasm, my significant shifter being very fond of both firearms and the color black.

The officers wore Coast Guard ballcaps and opaque black sunglasses. They did not smile.

While Leclerc filled them in, they turned black sunglasses toward us. I could see a funhouse version of Jean, Rene, and myself reflected in the lenses. What a trio of losers.

The next hour involved lies, followed by truths that sounded like lies, and ended with more lies. Rene and I stuck to the cousins-on-a-fishing-trip story, and Jean stuck to his pirate-on-a-tantrum story. Finally, the Coast Guard guys turned it over to the sheriff's deputies, who'd been joined by another water patrol boat carrying the sheriff himself. I recognized him from the news. He didn't smile, either.

They all conferred while the criminal, his wife, and his cousin sat on the deck.

Finally, Leclerc approached us. "Would you please stand, Mr. Breaux?"

Jean didn't move until I elbowed him. "That means you, honey."

We climbed to our feet, and I could feel the aura of Rene's nerves, which matched my own. They were going to arrest Jean; I had no idea what they'd do with Rene and me.

Jean silently turned around and allowed himself to be

handcuffed. I figured the silence wouldn't last long, however, and I was right.

Deputy Leclerc cleared his throat and turned Jean to face him. "Mr. Breaux, you have the right to remain silent."

"Pourquoi?" Jean gave me a quizzical look, and I placed a finger over my lips in a *shhh* gesture.

"Anything you say or do may be used against you in a court of law."

"Where shall this court be held? I do not feel—"

Leclerc glared at me, and I shrugged. What did he expect me to do? I poked Jean in the back with a forefinger and he shut up.

"You have the right to an attorney," Leclerc continued. "If you cannot afford an attorney, one will be appointed for you."

"I wish to have my attorney Edward Livingston brought here, *tout de suite, Jolie.*" Jean's glare in my direction joined that of Leclerc.

"No problem," I said, smiling. When hell froze over. As near as I recalled from my history lessons, Edward Livingston had been the pirate Lafitte's attorney in his human life. I had no intention of dragging an undead lawyer into this cluster.

Leclerc ground his teeth. "Do you understand your rights as I have explained them to you, Mr. Breaux?"

"Mais oui, Monsieur. Merci."

Oh *now* Jean was going to be charming, since he thought his undead lawyer would be sailing to his rescue.

Jean allowed himself to be shuffled to the other boat, where the sheriff himself awaited, then Leclerc returned to Rene and me. "From talking to Dr. Patterson and his students, it's clear the two of you were trying to de-escalate the situation, so you're free to go."

"What will happen to Jean? When can we see him?" I paused, then stated the obvious. "My husband is unwell."

"Are there medications he needs?"

I wondered if Xanax would work on the historical undead. "Nothing. He's been stable until today. The news about Lafitte's pirate ship being found really set him back."

Leclerc nodded. "I understand, ma'am. He'll be taken to the parish detention center for processing, then detained until an arraignment can be held. It's late on Friday, so he will likely be held at the parish jail until Monday. You should be able to visit him tomorrow."

Rene and I exchanged hangdog looks after bidding goodbye to Deputy Leclerc and watching a stoic Jean Lafitte sail away in handcuffs. I apologized to Dr. Patterson, then we headed back to *The Golden Girl*. Rene hoisted me over the rails without a single smartass comment.

In fact, he had only one observation before we began a silent trip back to our room in Cocodrie: "That pirate can get in a hell of a lot of trouble before tomorrow morning."

Never mind tomorrow. We had forty-eight hours to spring him from jail and get him back to the Beyond before he got his derrière hauled before a Terrebonne Parish judge.

The further he got into the justice system, the faster he'd be on his way to a psychiatric evaluation. They'd have him locked out of reach before we could say "historical undead."

Seven

AT THE COCO MARINA, Rene chewed on the last oyster from his massive Island Delight seafood platter and reached across the booth to take one of my soft shell crabs. I'd halfway eaten one, not having much of an appetite with my husband in jail and all.

"What you thinkin 'bout, babe? You been awful quiet." Rene broke off a crispy fried crab leg and stuck the whole thing in his mouth. "I been considerin' things, and Jean won't get in too much trouble. They'll just stick him in solitary if he gets outta control."

"That might be best, actually." I picked at my crab and bit the end off one of the legs. "I'm worried about the poor public defender that gets assigned to him; he might need memory modification." And possibly therapy.

"The main thing, though, is we need to get in there tomorrow and look at the security and setup so we can plan an escape," I added. "I'm not going to crawl to my boss and ask for help." I reported to the wizarding Elder who headed up all of North America. He would not be amused that I'd let the leader of the historical undead get arrested in Terrebonne Parish.

Rene grabbed a fistful of fries off my plate and dropped them onto his. "Can't you just make one of your little transports inside his jail cell and send him back to Barataria?"

I'd thought about that. "Yes, if they leave me alone with him, and if he's willing to go. Otherwise, I'll have to use some kind of potion or charm on the guard and figure out how to make Jean cooperate. He'll still want that damned ship. He's like a dog with a bone. A gator with a..." I had no idea what gators got fixated on.

"A gator with a rotten carcass," Rene said. "Gators got bad taste."

"How pissed off do you think Jean will get if I use a potion or charm on him?" My confusion charm was one of my most effective.

"It would work—until it wore off." Rene shook his head. "But he'd eventually try to come back for *Le Diligent.* Whatever we do, we need to do it now and get the hell out of here for good."

I'd come on this little mission hoping it would distract me from all the problems waiting at home. Funny how those problems no longer looked so insurmountable. I vowed to work harder at my relationship with Alex when I got back.

"You know, I got a look at that ship while I was diving." Rene paused to ogle the swaying hips of a young waitress in a pair of tight shorts as she walked by balancing a tray of food.

He didn't have time for a close encounter of the waitress kind. "Eyes back in your head, merman. What about the ship?"

"It's in better shape than I expected," he said. "It's sittin' upright, and looks pretty much intact. I want to go down tonight and look around in a half shift so I can use my hands."

Which fed into the scheme I'd been devising. "Why is Jean so keen to get this thing back? I mean, it isn't as if it's seaworthy. What's in there?" I'd bet my next few paychecks it was shiny and began with a *g* and ended with *old*.

"Gold, and lots of it." Rene waited while the waitress refilled our glasses. "Wrapped in a bearskin."

I stared at him. "A bearskin? And he thinks a bearskin has survived two centuries of seawater?"

Rene shook his head. "No, but the bearskin was stuffed inside a metal trunk in the ship's hold, under a trap door of some kind. Since the ship is mostly in one piece, it was probably in deep, cold water. He thinks the box could have survived."

Gold. I knew it. The pirate liked his money, and gold was worth a hell of a lot more now than in Jean's time, even allowing for inflation. "He won't let this go until he knows for sure. Is it safe for you to dive that deep at night in open water?"

Rene would never hear the term *agoraphobia* from me.

"Don't much like it, but I'll tie an anchor line and it'll be okay." He stuffed the last fry into his mouth and leaned back. It had taken more than an hour, but he finally seemed to be full. "I called the rental guy and paid to keep the boat until

Monday morning. I shouldn't need anything else."

"You sure? Can you can see in the dark?"

He gave me a look. "Babe, how many dolphins you see swimmin' around wearing night-vision goggles?"

I narrowed my eyes at him. "You don't have to be a smartass."

Rene smiled. "Yeah, I do."

THREE HOURS LATER, I sat shivering in *The Golden Girl* wheelhouse. We'd cruised around an hour after sunset, well after *Geaux Tiger* finally headed inland. Rene had anchored a few hundred yards east, far enough away to avoid suspicion in case the Terrebonne Parish Sheriff's Office or Coast Guard had anyone watching the wreck site.

It was black as sin out here, with the boat's only two lights heaving up and down to remind me how choppy the water had gotten—in case the heaving of the soft-shell crab in my stomach wasn't reminder enough. Tendrils of panic wrapped around my brain as I imagined what I might do if Rene didn't return. If a storm blew up, or if the anchor somehow got cut, or if the Gulf version of the many-legged Kraken arose from the deep and snatched me off the deck.

After all, I was a wizard who couldn't swim, stuck on a boat in the Gulf of Mexico in the middle of the night, waiting for a merman who was exploring an undead pirate's shipwreck from 1814. How outside the realm of possibility could the appearance of a mythical monster be?

Plus, it was cold. The soft sunlight had made the afternoon pleasant, but absent its warmth, the temperatures had plummeted. The brisk wind didn't help.

By the time I heard a big splash on the port side of the boat almost two hours later, I was so jumpy I remained huddled into the corner of the wheelhouse bench so the Kraken couldn't get me. When the thumps sounding on the same side didn't quite cover a familiar sneeze, however, I buttoned up my big-girl sweater and went outside in time to lean casually against the rail and watch Rene climb aboard.

He shook off water like a dog and grabbed his pants off the deck, giving me a closeup view of his impressive tattoos and the trim, muscular body they covered as he strode past me. Not that I was looking.

"It's cold out here, babe. Why you standin' outside?"

"Waiting for you." I followed him into the wheelhouse. "Besides, you're a shifter. You're never cold."

"Deep water ain't warm." He pulled on his clothes and flipped the switch to raise the anchor. With a jerking motion, *The Golden Girl* came back to life and I finally began to relax. He flipped another switch and warm air filtered into the cabin.

Who knew there was heat?

Rene didn't want to talk pirate until we got back to the room in Cocodrie, so we stuck to idle chitchat while he navigated the boat to the ramp, hitched it up to his truck, and drove us back to our rental rooms that seemed a lot emptier without the French pirate and his oversized personality.

Finally, we sat at the little dining table and divided a bag of potato chips. I couldn't stand it any longer; Rene's wonky shifter energy, which usually felt cold and buzzy on my skin, had amped from bumblebee to hornet. "What did you find?"

"I think it's there." He chewed the last chip and wadded up the plastic wrapper, aiming it at the trashcan and missing badly. So much for his basketball career. "Most of the stuff around the deck area is broken or missing, but Jean had told me where the trunk was hidden, and that flooring belowdeck is still mostly intact. I felt around and thought I could make out the edge of something solid like a trunk but it's too dark. Besides, bones are floatin' around in there."

"Bones?" I regretted the greasy chips. "You mean skeletons?"

He nodded. "Not whole ones. Just a few skulls and leg bones and shit. It's creepy."

Terrific. "How'd they survive this long?"

"Same way the ship did, I guess. It was in deep, cold water and got pushed in by that last tropical storm." Rene shrugged. "Who knows?"

"Can you swim back tomorrow night and bring out the trunk?"

He shook his head. "No way it's coming out of there without me tearing up the whole deck, and even with shifter strength that would take a while. They got divers down there taking pictures every day."

I wasn't worried about the cameras. Maybe the scientists wouldn't be able to explain what happened to a suddenly demolished lower deck, but they'd have a great geeky good time publishing papers on their theories.

"Forget the scientists. Our biggest problem is time." I retrieved a soda. "We've got to be finished by Sunday. Since it's a weekend, Jean's arraignment can't be held until Monday. We've got to spring him from jail and get the hell out of Terrebonne Parish before then."

Putting Jean Lafitte in front of a human judge would create a bigger mess than I'd be able to clean up without help. He'd lose his seat on the Interspecies Council at best. At worst, if he caused a big-enough ruckus, the Elders might confine him to the Beyond and keep him out of modern New Orleans altogether. His body might be immortal, but that would kill his spirit. I didn't even want to think what they'd do to me. The list of job options for de-licensed wizards was limited. I'd have to hand out carts at Walmart.

"We need to transport the whole ship then," Rene said. "Otherwise, as soon as we get back to Barataria, Jean's gonna end up trying to get that gold on his own. You know he ain't giving up."

Yeah, I knew. And God forbid Commodore Patterson's ancestor found it and claimed the gold for LSU, or the United States government claimed it, or France, or Spain. They might even fight over it; I'd be doing the international community a favor by making it disappear.

I'd never tried moving anything that large, but I wasn't sure mass was a factor in transporting anyway.

"Do you think if we did another power-share you could lay a big transport around the whole ship and send it to Old Barataria?" I asked Rene.

His eyes widened, and he pushed himself away from the table. He walked into his bedroom and returned with a bottle of bourbon. After the novelty had worn off, he hadn't liked the power-share any more than I. Plus, it had been part of the situation that ended with his twin brother's murder.

"I thought we agreed we wasn't ever goin' down that road again, babe. I don't even want to talk about it. Not after what happened to Robert." He unscrewed the top of the Jack Daniel's and took a swig straight out of the bottle. I had better manners; I went to get two coffee cups out of the little furnished kitchen and poured us both a healthy dose. Maybe it would help me sleep.

"I know you miss him." I shoved the coffee cup of bourbon toward Rene. "This trip's the first time you've mentioned him."

He sipped from the cup and stared into space. "This is the first diving I've done since then. I'd been afraid it would bring back too many memories, but damn if I didn't enjoy it. That seems wrong."

"No, it doesn't seem wrong, Rene. That's an important part of who you are." I paused. "I didn't know Robert that well, but from what I saw, this is exactly the type of adventure he'd have loved. He'd be all over this pirate ship thing."

Rene smiled and drained his cup. "Yeah, you right. I guess that's why he's been on my mind so much. Maybe that's good. It don't hurt so much to think about him out here, away from where we lived."

For the first time, I was glad we'd come. Maybe this would give my friend the closure he needed. Well, unless we lost Jean Lafitte in the process.

"Okay then, let's channel Robert for a while. What would be his solution to the pirate ship transport?"

Rene grinned. "He'd tell us to move the whole damned thing, and he'd be right."

I nodded. "Probably so. It's the only way we can make sure Jean will go home and stay put once we get him out of jail. If *Le Diligent* is in Old Barataria, he can plunder it to his heart's content."

Rene poured more bourbon into his coffee cup. "What're the LSU people gonna say when it disappears?"

I shrugged. "Who cares? They'll think it washed away, or it'll just add to all the mysteries about Jean Lafitte. If it's in the Beyond, we don't have to worry about them finding it."

For the next hour, we talked about our options and how the operation might work. I carried iron filings in my messenger bag, so we'd be able to lay a solid transport by figuring out how to embed the iron in the sea floor. On a napkin, I sketched out how *Le Diligent* might fit into the widest part of the triangle for the interlocking circle and triangle of a transport.

We could power it with blood instead of mercury.

"Uh oh." I turned to look at my backpack, which I'd set on the kitchen counter. During our earlier power-share, Rene had used charms I'd made ahead of time; he hadn't needed to actually do any magic. This situation was different.

In anyone's hand but mine, Charlie was an inert stick of carved wood. Would Rene have enough power to run a transport underwater if he could only draw on my pathetic wizard's physical magic? Even if he drained enough power to kill me, I doubted it would be enough.

Rene's gaze followed mine and understanding dawned. "That thing ain't gonna work for me, DJ."

"It might." Charlie had responded to my vocal commands before, but I'd never tried to get him to work for another person.

Rene walked to the counter, retrieved the elven staff, and aimed it at a chair like Zorro brandishing a sword. "Burn, baby. Show your daddy some flames."

Nothing happened.

"Charlie, follow Rene's commands." At my words, a few sparks flew off the end, Rene yelped, and the staff rattled to the floor.

"That damn thing burned me." He held up his right hand, which had turned bright red. He might have blisters. "That ain't gonna work, babe, which means there's only one other solution if we're gonna do this."

I got a sinking feeling—as in, sinking to the bottom of the

ocean. "What?"

"You're gonna have to dive."

Oh. My. God.

Eight

RENE AND I LEFT the cabin early, stopping at the Houma Walmart for some supplies, including a couple of knives and an apple for the power-sharing ritual in case we decided to do it. We also bought plenty of junk food, if not the food of champions then definitely the food of the insecure. Next, we hit a sporting goods store that opened early for the benefit of hunters, which we were—on the hunt for diving equipment.

I hadn't agreed to do the dive, only to let Rene buy the gear. Baby steps.

"Get something you can wear." I batted away a snorkeling mask he had been trying to fit on my face. "I haven't said I'd do this. It's suicide, and I'm too young to die." I'd almost died plenty of times in the last couple of years, but not by doing something as stupid as scuba diving.

"I ain't gonna let you drown, babe. Plus, I know CPR."

Yeah, his CPR is why I still had to tape my ribs every day. Deep inside, I knew me taking Charlie underwater was inevitable, but I didn't have to be mature about it.

In less than an hour, the back of Rene's truck was crammed

full of the scariest bunch of stuff I'd ever seen, including the undead serial killer known as the Axeman of New Orleans. Hoses tangled with air gauges and masks and fins and tanks.

Tanks, plural. If God had meant humans to breathe underwater, He wouldn't have invented merfolk.

I had to put fear of death by diving out of my mind, however. Our next stop was the Terrebonne Parish Criminal Justice Complex, where the local criminal justice officials had no clue how complex their lives had gotten last night with the arrival of Jean Lafitte, angry, undead, and in the flesh.

The building was sprawling, modern, and featured a lot of natural lighting, at least in the public areas. Accustomed to the ancient Orleans Parish courthouse at Tulane and Broad, where I periodically had to weasel out of jury duty, I found the place sterile and way too clean.

New Orleans was quirky, atmospheric, and a great place to live, but *sterile* and *clean*? Not so much.

Blue-uniformed officers sat at computer terminals inside an octagonal glass-walled cage. In front of them, embedded in the glass, were the kind of speakers one found at movie theaters in bad neighborhoods. I'd bet most of Jean Lafitte's gold the glass was bulletproof.

I took a deep breath and approached the nearest officer, with Rene trailing behind me. "Excuse me, but my husband was brought in last night and the deputies said I'd be able to see him this morning."

The round-faced officer, middle-aged and world-weary,

looked as if he'd seen every possible con job and criminal pass through this complex. He gave me a blank cop face. "Name?"

"Jane Breaux. My husband is Jean Breaux, like the former senator only spelled differently." I thought a moment. "At least that's his real name. He also might have claimed to be the pirate Jean Lafitte."

My face heated under the officer's sudden quirk of lips that might pass as a smile in Cop Land. "Oh, he's here. But I'm afraid Mr. Breaux has been uncooperative, so I'm not sure you'll be able to see him. Wait here."

Damn that pirate. Would it kill him to play nice for twelve freaking hours? Obviously.

The officer came back with an envelope and handed it to me: "Your husband's personal effects, and a receipt for the items we retained as evidence."

I took the envelope, curious as to what personal effects Jean had on him. It would have to wait.

"I'm so sorry. As I explained to Deputy Leclerc yesterday, my poor husband suffers from...episodes." Yeah, episodes of bad temper and excessive ego.

The officer tapped on his computer keyboard and looked at the screen. "We have scheduled an emergency psychiatric consult for Sunday afternoon, ma'am. Maybe you can see him after that."

All I had to do to bring forth tears was think of the humiliation I'd feel when I admitted to my boss and to Alex that I had lost the leader of the historical undead in the

Terrebonne Parish judicial system.

"Please." I blinked hard so the tears would roll down my cheeks. Damn, I was good. "Just for a few minutes. He'll be more cooperative once I talk to him."

Because I was going to threaten that pirate within an inch of his immortal life.

I could tell the officer was wavering. I batted my eyes a little. Standing behind me, Rene coughed. Or choked on a laugh.

"Who's he?" The officer frowned at Rene, who was spoiling my Oscar-worthy performance.

"My husband's cousin," I said, sniffling again to bring the officer's attention back to the poor, worried spouse. "He just drove me over because I'm so upset."

The officer sighed, clearly a good man who had no idea he was being played. "You can go back, but the cousin has to stay out here. Let me see your identification."

The officer got up and left his glass cage, glanced at my fake Jane Breaux driver's license, and handed it back to me. He looked much taller now that he wasn't hunched behind the computer screen, especially when he propped his hands on his hips and frowned at my messenger bag. "You can't take that purse in with you; leave it with the cousin. Do you have anything in your pockets?"

"No sir." I turned my pockets inside-out to prove they were empty, ignoring the lint that wafted toward the floor and praying the officer didn't frisk me. If he did even a half-assed job of it, he'd find Charlie strapped to my calf beneath my jeans, a confusion charm stuck in one shoe, and a sleep charm tucked in the other. A girl can't be too prepared.

Rene took my bag. "I'll wait on you in the truck. Tell Jean I said to keep his damn mouth under control or he's gonna miss deer season."

Yeah, that would break Jean's heart. He'd probably never even seen a deer. Then again, he apparently wrapped his gold in bearskins, so who knew.

I followed the officer down a long hallway. Away from the public entrance, the bright, shiny building morphed into a windowless, bland office complex. Eventually, if I went far enough, it would no doubt morph into windowless rows of jail cells.

The officer opened a door and motioned me inside. "Wait here. We'll bring him if he cooperates. If not, you'll have to wait until after the psych consult." Which translated, I'm sure, as *after he's pumped full of enough sedatives to fell a moose.* That might not be a bad thing, if human drugs worked on the historical undead. I wasn't sure.

Inside the beige room sat a metal table with a wood laminate top, metal folding chairs on either side, and a door opposite the one I'd entered. I sat in one of the chairs and waited.

About five minutes passed before I heard Jean in the hallway, having a spirited, if one-sided, argument about Spanish fruit. I definitely heard the words *orange* and

Spaniard. And he never had anything nice to say about Spaniards since he'd spent most of his human life plundering their ships.

The door opened, and he strode into the room, sending my empathic senses into overload with the force of his outrage. I closed my eyes and tried to squelch the urge to bray like a donkey, because the source of his anger was obvious.

They'd taken away the cord he used to tie back his shoulder-length, wavy black hair, but that wasn't the problem. The problem was his fluorescent orange jumpsuit with *Terrebonne Parish Prison* stamped on the back. The suit was tight across his shoulders and baggy across his hips, obviously not tailored for the pirate's athletic build, and the pants were three inches too short and flashing bare calf. He wore short white athletic socks someone had scrounged up for him. Obviously, his pirate boots had been confiscated. It wasn't an outfit designed to please a man as arrogant and aware of his good looks as my pirate.

Jean shifted his commentary from his guard to me. "Drusilla, a grievance must be made against these ruffians and thieves. They have stolen my clothing and given me only this...this...." He ran out of words.

"Ugly-ass orange jumpsuit?" I offered, always ready to help Jean with his command of modern English.

"*Oui, exactement.* I demand that you obtain my release, *tout de suite.* And you must know, a woman who allows her husband to remain in such conditions for an entire evening must face reprimand."

I leaned back in the chair and crossed my arms. "And you must know that, in this day and age, should a man reprimand his wife too much, said wife might leave her husband to enjoy a longer time in his prison cell wearing his ugly-ass orange jumpsuit."

The guard who'd accompanied Jean into the room listened to this exchange with no expression. Now that Jean and I were both in silent mode, he leaned over to fasten the handcuffs to a ring on the center of the table, which forced the irate pirate to sit down.

"You got half an hour," the guard said. "I'll be right outside. If I hear or see anything through that door that I should not hear or see, visitation will be ended. That includes shouting, moving of furniture, excessive use of profanity, or sexual activity. Do you understand?"

I nodded. "Not a problem." I had a confusion potion with Jean's name on it in my shoe, and I wasn't afraid to use it.

The guard stepped outside the door but left it open.

I reached out and took Jean's big, scarred hands in mine and the expression in his cobalt-blue eyes softened. "Are you okay?" I asked. "Did they hurt you?"

"*Non.* I am in a cell, but it is far better than that my brother Pierre endured years ago in the Calaboose prison of *Nouvelle Orleans.* And I am learning many new modern phrases, although some I do not understand. What does *mofo* mean?"

I looked down at our hands, trying to control my urge to

giggle. We had limited time, so I had to talk fast and steer him away from mofos. "I'll explain later. For now, please cooperate with anything the guards say. Later today or early tomorrow, you will meet with a psychiatrist—a doctor who wants to talk to you and see if you are sane. If he gives you pills, don't take them."

Jean's hair-trigger temper took a radical spike, sending a shiver across my spine. "I will not talk to such a mofo as—"

"You *will* talk to him, and for God's sake don't call anyone a mofo. It's very rude." I put some force behind my words, and Jean shut up. "You will be calm. You will be charming. You will tell him your name is Jean Breaux and that you are from Grand Isle." Thank God I'd had the foresight not to put his address at the Hotel Monteleone in New Orleans on his fake identification card.

"Earlier, you said I must tell them the truth." Jean assumed his spoiled brat tone. "Why can you not secure my freedom now? I demand that you do not tarry."

I waited a heartbeat to see if talking about freedom would alert the guard, but it didn't. "The plans have changed. Now I need you to be a polite, cooperative man named John Breaux from Grand Isle. Tell them you realize that you are not Jean Lafitte, although you admire him greatly."

This pleased the pirate, who did admire himself greatly.

"An attorney might visit you as well. You are to tell him the same thing. You are to apologize and say the events aboard the research ship with Dr. Patterson were a mistake and that you are very sorry for them."

The muscles in Jean's jaw clenched. "And if I refuse to do these things, Drusilla?"

"Then it will be hard for Rene and me to get you out of here tomorrow."

More clenching. "And why must my freedom wait until tomorrow? Do you know the mofos and *gendarmes* have told me I will have to ride on the back of a *taureau sauvage* at some location they call *Angola*? This cannot be tolerated." The last few words were punctuated by the bang of the handcuffs against the table.

The guard stuck his head in the door. "I hear sounds I do not like. Do we need to cut this visit short?"

"No sir. I'm sorry," I said quickly, shooting Jean a warning glare. "He's just upset that someone threatened to make him ride a bull at the Angola Prison Rodeo next year." I bit my lower lip to avoid laughing. Again.

"Could happen," the guard said, then disappeared back into the hall.

I leaned over and whispered. "So if you don't want to ride a bull in the prison rodeo wearing an ugly-ass orange jumpsuit, you will be polite and do exactly what I told you."

Jean leaned forward. "I will do this thing, but we must address your impertinence after we obtain my gold."

Whatever.

"Rene and I are taking care of the ship." I gave him a brief version of the plan, and got two raised eyebrows at the whole

DJ-goes-diving part.

"But you cannot swim, *Jolie*. You will sink to the bottom of the sea, and I shall miss you."

"How touching. See what I'm willing to do for you?" Never mind that it was only to save my job and my self-respect in the wizarding community.

He smiled. "The rule that we cannot engage in *l'activité sexuelle* is quite unfortunate, *n'est-ce pas?*"

Uh huh. *"Très malheureux,"* I assured him.

"Time's up." The guard reappeared in the doorway, and walked in to unhook Jean's handcuffs from the table.

"Might I kiss my wife farewell?" Jean asked.

The guard looked at me, apparently taking my *please-no* look for a *please-yes*. "Keep it brief."

God help me. I'd kissed Jean before. More than once, in fact. He had wandering hands, so at least the handcuffs would prevent an inappropriate ass-grab. We exchanged smiles as I rose on my tiptoes and placed my hands on his shoulders. "No tongue," I whispered.

"Bah. Very well."

He cheated.

Nine

I STOOD IN THE bedroom of the cabin in Cocodrie in my underwear, trying to figure out how to get into the black neoprene wetsuit Rene had picked out for me. He admitted he bought it based on its sex appeal rather than practicality, which is what I get for letting a merman pick out anything I might want to wear.

I'd tried stepping into the thing and pulling it up, but ended up falling in the floor. Asking for Rene's help? Not happening.

The wetsuit, I finally concluded, was like rubber pantyhose for the whole body, so I rolled it up as best I could, stuck my feet through the leg holes, and shimmied it up. At some point, I lost my balance again. This time, having anticipated this likelihood, I'd started my shimmy near the bed and squirmed the rest of the way in a supine position.

Once I got the bottom in place, the top was easy—except for the whole so-tight-I-couldn't-breathe part. When I looked in the mirror, even that didn't bother me. I looked damn good in black neoprene, to my surprise. Who needed to breathe?

"Still not promising I'm going to do this," I reminded Rene, joining him in the cabin's den. "We don't know for sure that Charlie will even work underwater."

Rene and I had stayed up most of the night planning for any glitch we could think of, and had decided it was best not to do the power-share at all. He'd have access to my magic, but it would weaken me and I might need all my firepower to spring Jean from jail, depending on whether or not he managed to behave himself for another twenty-four hours.

I had my doubts.

Silence filled the truck as we headed to the boat ramp just before sunset, after which we spent a tense, quiet ride to the same spot we'd anchored the night before. This was a risky venture, and we'd said all there was to say. I'd never tried to transport anything the size of a ship to the otherworld, never mind from underwater. The only other time I'd been in water over my head, I'd drowned in the Mississippi River and had rib-cracking CPR from Rene. Robert Delachaise had died less than an hour earlier.

We both had a lot to think about.

It had rained during the day, and the water was choppier than ever. The wind whipped my hair around my face and forced me to pull it back in a ponytail. On the plus side, the neoprene was warm and didn't restrict my movement now that I'd gotten used to not breathing.

Rene had strapped on a neoprene backpack containing the iron filings that I'd encased in hollow tubing. Lots and lots of hollow tubing—enough to form a triangle, and then an interlocking circle, around *Le Diligent*.

"Let's walk through the equipment again, babe." Rene held up the twin tanks. "Put all this shit on so I'm sure you know how to do it."

I strapped on the tanks and the buoyancy thingamajig, then the face mask. Next, I strapped on the harness we'd devised to hold the staff. Finally, after slipping my feet into the fins, I popped the regulator into my mouth and pantomimed a dive into the water.

"Good job. You got it," Rene said, tugging off his sweater. "Once I get the transport laid out, I'll resurface. You jump in, and we'll swim in tandem after that."

"Sounds good." I hated to tell him, but he'd be swimming and I'd be letting him pull me along. My only goals were to avoid drowning and not lose the staff. Actual swimming wasn't even on my agenda.

And any debt I owed to Jean was paid in full if we managed to pull this off.

Rene finished undressing, checked to make sure the backpack was in place, and dove off the aft deck of *The Golden Girl*. He gave me a thumbs-up, barely visible in the dark water, then disappeared.

I figured it would take him at least an hour to lay out the transport and make sure it was secure, so I went back into the wheelhouse to think about Alex. After years of flirting around the edges, we'd taken a big step toward a committed relationship right before Thanksgiving. Yet our differences still threatened to pull us apart. Our physical attraction couldn't hold us together if we couldn't solve the deep issues, the ones that mattered.

This trip was a perfect illustration of our biggest stumbling block. Alex followed the rules, and I followed my heart. My heart had told me I owed Jean my life. If I couldn't talk him out of his attempt to retrieve his ship, as his friend I needed to help him.

We were breaking all kinds of wizarding laws: unlawful interference into human affairs (involving law-enforcement, no less); theft; risk of exposure to humans—and this was *before* I sprang Jean out of jail.

I hadn't told Alex about my plans, not because he was out of town but because his absence meant he'd never have to know. Such was not the transparency upon which one built a mature relationship.

I pondered such depressing matters for another half hour, then strapped on my gear and fin-flopped my way to the aft deck to wait for Rene. What would Alex say about me, a woman who was afraid of water, agreeing to dive into the Gulf of Mexico at night in order to transport a shipwreck to Jean's corner of the otherworld?

He'd use words I couldn't repeat in polite company, that's what. He'd also have a few words to say about my inability to say no to the pirate, and probably quite a diatribe about how Rene and I should not be allowed to go anywhere together again, ever. For me it was as simple as friendship. Friends helped friends, even when it wasn't the wisest course of action.

"Yo, DJ!"

I squinted into the darkness and finally spotted Rene bobbing in the black water. After waving to show I'd seen him, I double-checked my gear and made sure the makeshift harness securely held the staff in place.

Was I really going to do this? Bottom line: I trusted Rene to make sure I didn't die. At least not here, not tonight.

Right.

I took a regular breath, as per instructions, clamped the regulator between my teeth and, saying a quick prayer, propelled myself backward off the rail of *The Golden Girl.* The single light from the boat swirled and spun until I hit the water hard and went under...and panicked.

I scrambled for the surface, but Rene was already beside me, holding me up with one arm around my waist. With his other hand, he pulled out the regulator and I gulped in deep lungsful of air.

"Slow your breathing down, babe. You're okay." He was patient and waited until the panic subsided before handing me the regulator again. "Pop this in and breathe. Get used to breathing from the tank."

I nodded and did as he said. Once I got used to the bottled air, it wasn't so bad.

"Okay, hold out your hand and take this line."

I hadn't noticed it from the deck, but heavy yellow cord

stretched from the back of the boat and disappeared into the water. I raised my eyebrows in question.

"It goes all the way to the edge of the transport, where I have it tied off. If for some reason we get separated, just reach for that line, babe, and you can pull yourself to the surface. We're not going deep enough for you to get the bends so you'll be fine. Got it?"

I nodded. I wasn't going far from that line.

"Okay, put your arms around my neck from behind and hang on. We're gonna swim."

Yeah, easy for him to say. I focused on my breathing and wrapped my arms around Rene's neck from behind in such a death grip that he had to loosen my hands a little. "Babe, if you choke me, we're both gonna drown."

"Mwa mwa." It was as close as I could get to *ha ha* without unclamping my teeth from the regulator.

I closed my eyes as I felt him slip beneath the water, and then held on for dear life as he straightened his body out and swam like an aquatic horse carrying a frightened rider. He angled downward slowly, or at least I thought so, and I gradually relaxed as I realized my full body weight rested on his back. The big dorsal fin stretched beyond my feet.

When I finally dared to open my eyes, thanks to the light strapped to my left arm shining from beneath Rene's neck, I saw the faint outline of the yellow line to our right, within easy reach. This might work.

Now that my panic had subsided, I adjusted my arm so that

I could see a little of what lay around us. Mostly, it was murk, but occasionally I'd glimpse a fish or something flash past so quickly I couldn't recognize it.

Suddenly, the sea floor stretched before us. I'd expected a smooth expanse of sand, but the seabed was rocky and uneven. My small light picked up shallows and deeper areas, plus a lot of junk: pieces of metal, a square cage, bits of netting. Rocks and more rocks.

Rene reached back and tapped my hip to get my attention, then pointed ahead, where something massive loomed: *Le Diligent.*

I clutched his neck harder with my right arm and risked holding my left out to the side so I could control the light. The ship lay tilted on one side of its hull, the masts broken off, most of the deck collapsed.

Rene pointed to the left, and I saw what looked like a cannon half embedded in the sea floor—torn off the deck, maybe. That's what Rene had tied the end of the yellow line to.

As we'd agreed beforehand, Rene swam left and low, tracing the outline of the transport so I could check it all the way around. It seemed to take forever, but I willed myself to stay calm, breathe normally, and concentrate on the work he'd done. I found a small break near where he'd laid the circle to lock with the triangle, and watched while he repaired it. Then we returned to the yellow line and the edge of the transport nearest it.

Showtime.

Careful not to lose my grip on Rene, I fumbled around with my left hand until I finally found Charlie. I grasped the staff and tried an experimental shot at a random spot on the seabed. Instead of the red ropes of flame that usually shot from the staff, these flew out in electric blue—cold fire rather than hot.

I tapped Rene on the shoulder to let him know I was ready, and he swam to the nearest edge of the transport, where he'd placed the vial containing some of my blood. Aiming at the vial, I sent a mental command to Charlie: *Transport to Old Barataria.*

As I'd hoped, the power shot from the staff to the vial of blood and the blue light spread along the edges of the transport in both directions. Once it met in the middle on the other side, *Le Diligent* should disappear, rematerializing inside the transport near Jean's house on Grand Terre Island.

There was no doubt at what moment the magical fuse connected. An explosion of mud and sand and rocks flew outward, knocking me away from Rene and obscuring all vision.

I had no idea where I was or how far I'd been thrown.

Ten

A CRUNCHING NOISE AWOKE me, and I sat up with a groan. What the hell was Alex eating? And why had my dreams been filled with...

Oh. The fact that I was encased in a wet neoprene bodysuit brought everything back. I'd been stretched out on the bench at the rear of *The Golden Girl* wheelhouse, and the crunching noise was Rene, eating the Walmart apple.

"What happened? Did I need CPR again?" If so, he'd done a better job this time because my rib pain hadn't increased.

"No, I found you sitting on the ocean floor with your eyes closed. I think you were in shock or were meditating or doing yoga, but at least you kept the mouthpiece in."

Thank God for small favors. "What about the ship? Did it transport?" Leave it to me to do yoga in a cloud of mud and miss the whole thing.

Rene grinned. "It's gone, babe. I went back down after I hauled your ass back on the boat, and there's nothing down there but the cannon. Those LSU dudes are gonna be some freaked out."

"Too bad we can't see their faces." I looked around and didn't spot Charlie. "Rene, you've got to dive again. I lost—"

"Your magic stick? I got it." He held up the staff, then tossed it to me. "Better change so you'll warm up faster. You're shaking—of course, maybe you're still scared." Rene tossed my jeans and sweater at me and made no attempt to give me any privacy.

"Whatever." I was too cold to change on the deck and too tired to climb down the tiny stairway into the hold, so I shucked off the wetsuit and pulled on my clothes over my half-soaked underwear. Not comfortable but warmer.

"Let's get back to Cocodrie and find some food," I told him, throwing the wetsuit on the bench and looking around for the rest of the gear. "We have a prison break to plan."

An hour later, we were back at the CoCo Marina, stuffing down baked oysters and gumbo and crawfish pies. Now that my seafaring adventures were at an end, my appetite had returned. Besides, I needed my strength. Tomorrow would be an epic day, featuring what I hoped was a smooth, uneventful jailbreak.

We polished off our dinners and waited for the check for an awfully long time. Looking around for our waitress, I noticed most of the staff crowded around a TV set in the bar. "Wonder what's going on?"

"Dunno." Rene craned his neck to see the television. "Looks like something's on fire. You ain't been near anything else with that staff, have you?"

"Funny." It had been at least two weeks since I'd accidentally started a fire. In fact, the last thing I'd burned had been my own SUV.

Our waitress noticed us looking her way and hurried over to bring the check. "Sorry about that. Not often we have a full-on riot at the parish jail."

My hand froze halfway to the check. "Excuse me?"

"Oh yes, the whole place is on lockdown. There's a fire and teargas and all kinds of things going on."

I didn't dare look at Rene, but slid enough cash under the edge of the saucer to cover the bill and the tip. Then I hurried out the front door.

Rene was right behind me. "Think it's possible this has nothing to do with the pirate?"

I climbed in the passenger seat of the pickup and slid my gaze around to meet his; he looked as pale as I felt. "Theoretically, it's possible. You think maybe Jean's not involved?"

He cranked the truck and peeled rubber as he pulled out of the parking lot, headed north toward Houma. "Hell no. He's up to his French eyeballs in the middle of that shitstorm."

I couldn't have said it better.

We failed to get within three blocks of the Criminal Justice Complex, which had been cordoned off with an array of vehicles from every law enforcement agency imaginable, even Louisiana Wildlife and Fisheries. I hope Jean wasn't adding trout abuse to his list of crimes.

A Houma P.D. officer stopped us as we tried to edge closer. Rene rolled down his window and I leaned across. "Officer, my husband's in there. Can you tell us if anyone's been hurt?"

He flashed his light inside the cab of the truck but apparently didn't see anything threatening. "Sorry, ma'am, but I don't have any information. Does your husband work for the parish? If so you might call the sheriff's office."

I didn't think it would be helpful to say my pretend husband was a prisoner and quite possibly the cause of the riot, so I settled for a polite thank you.

"What now, babe? We ain't getting anywhere near that place till they get it under control."

"I could slip in using a camouflage potion. Maybe." Or maybe not. Even if I had enough ingredients to make confusion charms for the entire population of Terrebonne Parish, it might not get me through that maze of guards and prisoners.

Rene and I had planned to visit Jean in the morning and, if possible, I would simply transport us both from the visitation room straight to the transport I'd created in the bed of Rene's truck.

That plan might be out the window.

"What if they kill him?" Rene asked. "You know how annoying Jean gets. Hell, I want to kill him at least once a week and he's one of my best friends."

I knew the feeling. "If they kill him, he'll disappear and end up back at his house in Barataria, needing to heal all over again. But there would be hell to pay from the Elders. No way we're going to know what's happening to him without getting in that prison."

Except there was. Damn it, I could scry him.

"What you thinkin', wizard? I can see trouble all over your face."

I took one last look at the flames rising from the direction of the jail. "Take me to Walmart."

An hour later, I sat at a faux wooden table in a Houma Days Inn room, forming a scrying station with my purchases. I set a dark-colored glass bowl in the center of the table, and around it placed items I'd found in Jean's personal-effects: a small pen knife the deputies must have decided didn't qualify as a weapon, a leather pouch holding gold coins that must constitute his emergency funds, an old-fashioned key that opened only God knew what, and a condom.

I didn't want to know.

Placing those at north, south, east and west around the bowl, I next settled four small votives beside each of Jean's items.

Then I waited for Rene, who'd left immediately after dropping me off. His job? Retrieving our stuff from Cocodrie and then breaking into a Catholic church. He needed to steal enough holy water for the scrying ritual.

There were no TV stations in Terrebonne Parish, so I stretched out on the bed nearest the door and watched the ten o'clock news out of Baton Rouge, where the Terrebonne jail riot rated exactly one minute of airtime. I learned three things during that minute, however: first, the riot had been contained; second, the prisoner credited with starting the riot, which seemed to have started when he attacked a fellow inmate following an argument about the 19th-century pirate Jean Lafitte, would be transported to the maximum-security penitentiary in Angola after his arraignment on Monday morning; and third, the culprit was, indeed, my pirate.

Footage showed a tall, longhaired man in handcuffs and shackles being hustled down a prison corridor, having a vigorous conversation with his guards, who were ignoring him with stoic faces. The newscaster added that the prisoner appeared to speak little English.

Actually, he spoke plenty of English but only when he chose to do so. Where were they taking him?

A sharp knock on the door sent me jumping out of my skin, such was the state of my nerves. I opened it to find an irate merman.

He thrust a gallon glass jar into my arms. The liquid in it was green-tinged, and the label on the front said *Vlasic Large Whole Dills*. "Did you rinse this out?" I didn't know how holy water and pickle juice would work for scrying.

"No, I did not rinse this out." Rene sent a bite-me look in my direction. "I had to go to the damned Rouse's on the other side of town, then pour out the damned pickles. Then I had to spring the damned backdoor lock on St. Matthew the Apostle, which set off a damned alarm. *Then* I had to find where they'd stashed their holy water and get out of there before the police drove up, which they did about a second after I rounded the corner to leave. Then I had to go back down to Cocodrie and get our stuff and leave the boat keys for the owner.

"So no, I did not rinse out the damned pickle jar." He flopped on the other bed. "And since I'll be going to hell for breaking into a church and stealing holy water, I'll be sure to mention your name when I get there." He paused. "You're probably on Satan's wish-list anyway."

"Thanks." He could be right, especially if chaos was considered a sin. I took the jar to the table and poured the vinegar- and dill-scented holy water into the bowl. It made me crave pickles. "By the way, Jean is on his way to Angola after his arraignment."

Rene pulled a pillow over his head. "Don't say another word to me about that pirate, babe. We should leave him there until the rodeo. He deserves to get bounced off the back of a bull."

I had to admit the image was tempting, but I was worried about the pirate. He couldn't be killed—at least not permanently. As a member of the historical undead, he'd go back to the Beyond and heal. But he felt pain like anyone else. He could be injured, and if he'd gotten into a fight to set off the prison riot, it might have reopened that wound on his chest. The one I had caused.

I wouldn't let him be hauled off to Angola and neither would Rene. We'd just find a bull when we got home and make him ride it for our own enjoyment.

Taking Charlie from my backpack, I settled the end of the staff into the water and waited for the swirl of mist to dissipate. Rene must have absolved me of my sins, because I felt him peering over my shoulder.

In the scried image, Jean sat at a table across from a high school student.

"Who the hell is that kid?" Rene pulled up a chair so he could see better.

"Well, the guy looks about twelve, but he has a briefcase, so it might be Jean's public defender." That poor child wouldn't stand a chance.

"Jean looks pretty beat up."

I adjusted Charlie's angle so we could get a better look at Jean's face. He was uncharacteristically silent, and was giving Doogie Lawyer his best stony look. Scratches and cuts covered his face, and a deep turquoise bruise bloomed on his jawline. He seemed to be clutching his midsection.

"He's holding a hand over his injury from last month." I studied Jean's face, looking for any wince of pain or sign that he'd been drugged, but his eyes pierced Doogie Lawyer with their usual clear cobalt. "I think he's just pouting."

"Yeah, he ain't hurt; he's pissed off," Rene said. "I know that look. He's making plans. We need to get him out of there tonight before he get in more trouble."

"I don't think so. Security's going to be insane tonight." Tomorrow was Sunday, and if Jean could make it through the rest of the night without incident, things might relax a bit.

The day would be busy with families visiting inmates, making it easier for me to slip in with Charlie and some charms. "Hopefully, they'll throw Jean in solitary confinement and let him stew for the next few hours."

"Then I'm going to sleep. That swim wore me out, never mind church burglary." Rene managed to shed his clothes before reaching the bed, leaving them in the floor like a trail of breadcrumbs. He pulled the spread over his head and his breathing relaxed into an easy rhythm.

I watched Jean a while longer. No point in trying to read his lips since he wasn't talking. Doogie Lawyer's face was a study in frustration. I had no doubt he wanted to plead mental illness, but it would be hard to do with a client who refused to talk.

Finally, Doogie Lawyer stood up and held his hand out to shake with Jean. The pirate looked at the hand, looked up at the young man, and gave him a smile that sent shivers across my shoulder blades.

It brought to mind a story from Jean's human life. One of his men had fomented rebellion among those who'd pledged loyalty to the Lafittes, then made the mistake of telling Jean to his face. Jean pulled out his pistol and shot the man without a word. I imagined he might have been wearing a smile much like the one he'd just given Doogie Lawyer.

The earlier we got there in the morning, the better.

Eleven

GOOD THING RENE COULD sleep since he was having to sleep for two. My brain spun like a hamster on a tilt-a-whirl, so I spent the evening dismantling my magic supplies and making as many potions and charms as I had materials to create. Since Charlie could handle any fires that needed setting, I focused on basics: confusion charms, sleep-inducing charms, and illusions.

I'd focused my energy and supplies on charms because they were more effective for fieldwork. They deployed on impact near the face and could be thrown from a distance, assuming my aim was good. Never mind that it usually wasn't.

The camo potion, which tasted like dirty socks, Rene and I would have to drink.

I also kept an eye on Jean throughout the night. After Doogie Lawyer left with his shoulders slumped inside his oversized suit and his shuffle resembling that of an 80-year-old man, his silent, scheming client had been escorted to a solitary cell with a solid door instead of bars. He'd kicked the wall several times—his jailers had scrounged up some loafers somewhere. He paced a lot. He examined the door hinges with great interest, as if perhaps he might break himself out. Finally, he'd curled up on the bunk, facing the wall. After an hour, I got tired of watching him get more sleep than me and stared until dawn at infomercials with the volume turned off.

The woman who answered the phone at the Criminal Justice Complex at six a.m. said visiting hours didn't start until ten, but Rene was an early riser due to his normal schedule as a commercial fisherman and I'd never gone to bed. We packed up and left the hotel at seven, planning to dawdle over breakfast and continue our argument over whether he'd stay outside with the getaway truck or go inside with me.

"Your boobs are kinda lumpy, babe." He frowned at me as he got in the truck, having finally agreed to man the getaway vehicle. "Might want to do something about that."

I'd stuffed my bra with the little vials of potions and charms, figuring they'd search my messenger bag and maybe my pockets. Lumpy boobs would probably be suspect as well, though.

After climbing in the truck, I stuck my hand down the neck of my sweater, retrieved half of them, and stuffed them into my socks. Then I patted the rest into cleavage-hiding, non-lumpy spots. Rene watched with way too much amusement.

"What?" I hadn't heard him offering to hide anything.

"I was just thinkin' how much the pirate would have dug watching that." Shaking his head, he drove downtown and pulled into the parking lot of a Waffle House three blocks from the Criminal Justice Complex.

We sat in a booth next to the front window and ate mostly in silence, downing enough coffee to ensure I wouldn't sleep for a week. There was no planning to be done. If I could see Jean, I'd transport with him out of the visiting room to the bed of Rene's truck. If I couldn't visit him, I'd have to wing it.

A few minutes before ten, we made the short drive to the jail. Rene dropped me off at the building's front door and went to park the truck in a side lot still crowded with law-enforcement vehicles. So much for being light on staff this Sunday morning. No telling how much paperwork Jean's behavior had generated.

I waited near the door forever, or at least long enough for Rene to have parked and crawled on all fours from Cocodrie. Call me paranoid, but I had a bad feeling. Walking around the corner of the building so I could see the parking lot, I spotted the merman arguing with a police officer. They seemed to be arguing about the truck.

I wandered in their direction but before I'd gotten too close, Rene caught my gaze and gave me a subtle head shake. I stayed a hundred or so yards away, leaned against a car, closed my eyes, and opened my senses. It was a technique I often used to sense preternatural energy and read others' emotions, but I'd also found it effective for eavesdropping.

"I'm tellin' you, I ain't been near a church in ten years, me. Just don't be tellin' my mama." Rene had his Cajun accent turned to its heaviest setting, no doubt to improve his local credibility. "Besides, if I done robbed a church, you think I'd be stupid enough to drive to da parish jail and hang out in da parkin' lot?"

Holy crap, no pun intended. Rene said the cops had spotted his truck as he left the church, but that they hadn't gotten close enough to get his license plate number. If they found fingerprints, though, they'd be able to match them to Rene and then a simple license-plate check would give them his real name and address.

Worse—did merfolk even have the same type of fingerprints as humans? Rene and the whole Delachaise clan mainstreamed so well, I'd never thought to ask.

An eighteen-wheeler rumbled its way down the block, drowning the sound of their voices. I edged a little closer.

"—is fine, but you're wastin' both our time," Rene was saying when the truck finally got out of range. He'd already begun walking with the officer toward the back door of the complex, in the opposite direction from where I stood.

Damn it, Rene was about to get himself arrested too. I ran after them, but before I could catch up, confusion charm at the ready, they'd already gone inside. I tried the back door, but it had locked behind them.

Great. Now I had two convicts to rescue.

Before I figured out the logistics of the latest cluster in a road trip full of them, I needed to do some precautionary damage control. Opening one of the vials of illusion charm I'd tucked into the side of my shoe, I spread a thin layer of the noxious liquid over Rene's license plate and used a bit of my own physical magic to change two digits in the number.

Like most charms, it had a short shelf life—two or three hours, maybe—but if the officer hadn't written down the number and came back for it, he'd get the wrong one. The truck was locked, so I couldn't change the VIN. It was the best I could do unless I used Charlie to set the truck on fire, which Rene might consider overkill.

I sat on the curb for a few minutes, wondering how to get Rene out as well as Jean. The merman hadn't been arrested—at least not yet—so he'd probably be taken to a different wing of the sprawling complex.

Jean's situation was more dire and his temperament more volatile, so I decided to get him squared away first and then go on the hunt for Rene. With any luck, by the time I got Jean out, Rene would already be back at his truck.

Returning to the complex's lobby, I pasted on a perky smile and approached the first available officer, a red-haired woman with a friendly face. "I'd like to visit my husband, please. Jean Breaux."

Her face didn't stay friendly for long; it grew downright hostile in a matter of seconds. Jean was making friends and winning over enemies as usual. "I'm afraid Mr. Breaux is not allowed visitors, ma'am. You will be able to see him at his arraignment tomorrow."

I tried to summon more tears, but fatigue and stress had dulled my acting skills. Instead, I went for Plan B:

belligerence. I could always do belligerent. It came naturally to most wizards.

"This is absurd." I propped my hands on my hips and raised my voice. "I haven't been allowed to see my poor husband since yesterday, and he was brought in with an injury that needs medical attention. Has he gotten medical attention? Can you assure me he has his medications? He also has psychiatric problems. Has he gotten a psychiatric evaluation and, if so, why was I, his wife, not informed? I don't even know if he's been provided with the attorney we were promised."

Officer Sourpuss was not impressed by theatrics, apparently, although I'd amassed a small following of onlookers among the visitors. She clicked on her keyboard a few times, scribbled something on a slip of paper, and handed it to me through a narrow slot at the bottom of the glass. "There's his lawyer's name and a phone number. Thank you, ma'am. Next person, please?"

Summarily dismissed, I looked at the paper. Doogie Lawyer's real name was Michael Fonseca, and his day was about to get a lot worse.

Twelve

Turned out that Michael Fonseca, accent on the "fon," wasn't as immune to the rants of a hysterical spouse as Officer Sourpuss. I only got halfway through my spiel before he interrupted in a voice that bordered on excitement, promising to be at the jail in half an hour.

He made it in twenty minutes, and looked even younger and more trusting in person. "Call me Mick," he said, shaking my hand.

Mick was tall, with pretty blond hair, sky-blue eyes, and a look of eager sincerity that was, by the time I finished with him, going to be squashed like a bug. I'd feel guilty later.

"Mick, have you met with my husband? Can you help him?"

This was Mick's first test, to see if he was as innocent as he looked.

He was. "Mrs. Breaux—can I call you Jane?" I nodded. "Jane, I tried to talk to him last night after the, uh, incident, and he wouldn't say a word. I have to tell you, the way he looked at me..." Mick fixed his gaze on the floor. "It's going to be hard for me to help him."

I saw my opening.

"See, he gets that way sometimes," I said, shaking my head in mock sadness. "If they'd let me talk to him, I could convince him to cooperate with you. Right now, he feels alone and abandoned, so he's shut himself off. But they won't let me see him."

My acting skills had returned with a vengeance.

"I will make it happen," Mick said, all brisk confidence. "It's necessary for his legal defense."

Sounded good to me.

I followed him across the lobby of the Justice Center Complex, where two officers were currently unoccupied. One was Sourpuss. "Don't go to her," I whispered, steering him to the left. "Try the other one."

It took conversations with four different officers, each a bit more authoritative than the last, but Mick finally prevailed. His grin was so wide when he motioned me to follow him, I couldn't help but grin back despite what I was about to do to the poor kid.

The final officer on the food chain—the one who'd given the okay—could have been an NFL player. He was so tall and broad that his shoulders stretched the fabric of his blue uniform shirt. He led us down a hallway and into a round central desk area surrounded by a series of doors that looked like solid steel. Into each door had been inset a small window of double-paned safety glass.

Jingling a hefty set of keys, the officer, whose uniform

identified him as J. Jones, unlocked the door on the far end, just before the cell area ended in a solid wall of tan-painted concrete blocks. They'd gotten Jean as far away from polite society as possible. Probably a smart idea.

"I'm going to close the door once you get inside; this prisoner has a history of disruptive behavior." Officer Jones addressed his comments to Mick, ignoring me. "I will be in the central guard area until you knock three times to let me know you are ready to leave. If this is not acceptable, you can wait and speak to him before his arraignment tomorrow."

Mick looked around at me and I nodded. Jean Breaux was not the one Mick needed to fear; it was his short blond wife, Jane. Poor kid.

"We're fine with that, officer, thank you." Mick straightened his suit jacket. His mama really needed to get that tailored for him; the blue pinstripe hung off his shoulders like they were coat hangers.

I followed him into the room, struck with sadness at seeing my friend Jean so beaten up, even if he had brought it on himself. He sat on his bunk, his jaw now a deep purplish-blue, his eyes dull. I wondered if they had drugged him after all.

Then he saw me, and his whole demeanor changed. "*Jolie*! You have come for me at last."

Jean rose from his bunk slowly, holding a hand over his belly. He didn't seem to be drugged, but he had reinjured that wound.

"You know I wouldn't leave you here longer than I had to." I hugged him and whispered, "Play along. I'm getting you out of here."

"Merci, Jane." He kissed my cheek and released me.

"Do you remember your attorney, Mick Fonseca?" That would be Mick the Innocent, who'd flashed a big smile at his undead client. "He's the one who got me in to see you."

"Mais oui. My great thanks to you, *monsieur."* Jean bowed in a courtly gesture and Mick held a hand out to shake, then jerked it back, then bowed in return. The kid was way in over his head.

"Monsieur Fonseca, might I ask that you allow me to speak with my wife alone for a few moments?" Jean gave him a friendly smile. "I assure you that I have a great deal of money and will reward your efforts to be helpful."

My empathic senses registered Mick's confusion. "What? I thought this was an indigent case. If you have money, why are you using the public defender's office?"

Jeez, I wish Jean wouldn't go off-script. I gave Mick a quick headshake. "My husband sometimes believes he is the wealthy privateer Jean Lafitte," I whispered. "We are quite poor, believe me. You are our only hope."

"Bah." Jean sat on his bunk again and I went to sit beside him, sizing up the best way to establish a transport in the room.

"I understand completely." Reassured that he was doing his part to defend the defenseless, Mick grabbed the folding chair

Officer Jones had provided and pulled it close enough to sit on while resting his briefcase on the bunk next to Jean.

While he flipped through papers and yammered about defense strategies, I got up, pulled an envelope of magicked sea salt from my left shoe, and began laying out a small interlocking circle and triangle. Salt transports didn't last more than a few hours, but if we needed more time than that, something had gone terribly wrong.

Jean did his part by distracting Mick. "I very much enjoy the tailoring of the suit you are wearing, Monsieur Fonseca. Is it by any chance French? Fonseca is a fine old French name, of course. Are your people natives of this part of *Louisiane?*" And on he went, talking nonstop until the transport was finished and Mick wore an expression as dazed as if I'd used a confusion charm on him.

"Jean, would you come here, please? I feel the need to give you a hug."

My faux-spouse winced when his wide grin caused a cut on his lip to reopen. *"Assurément, Jolie."*

Mick looked around. "You need to hug now? Why? We need to prepare his defense."

I stuck a hand down the front of my sweater and dug around for one of the sleep charms hidden in my bra—an action that, as Rene anticipated, Jean seemed to find quite interesting. Flipping the top off the vial, I said, "Sorry, Mick," and flicked a few drops in his face.

I hadn't given him a full dose because I might need him to

retrieve Rene, but it was enough to earn an immediate yawn so he must be really susceptible to the effects of magic. "I don't know what…" he mumbled, and then tumbled forward. Quick movement on Jean's part guided him onto the bunk, fast asleep.

"Okay, let's get out of here."

Jean looked toward the door. "Where is Rene?"

"Long story. Let's transport to the truck first."

I pulled Charlie from under the straps around my calf and powered the transport as Jean stepped in beside me. I whispered, "Rene's truck."

The suck of compressing space reminded me that my ribs were still healing, but within a second, we were in the back of the pickup—which was still in the Justice Complex parking lot, with no sign of Rene. Damn it.

I turned to Jean, who'd already jumped out of the truck bed. "Look, Rene's gotten in a little trouble—nothing major—but I need to go back in and get him. You can't stay out here where you'd be spotted, so I need you to transport back to Barataria now."

"*Non, Jolie.* Rene is my dear friend. Jean Lafitte does not leave his friends."

That was a fine and dandy principle when one wasn't standing outside the jail where one had recently caused a riot—a story I had yet to hear from the main combatant. "Jean." I kept my voice calm. "*Le Diligent* is at Barataria, waiting for you. Don't you want to see her again?"

"Drusilla." He spoke as if to a child, mimicking my tone. "*Le Diligent* will not sail away on her own. I will see her once we have retrieved Rene." He climbed back into the truck bed and stepped into the transport. "Let us go. *Tout de suite.*"

We were wasting too much time. "Jean's jail cell," I muttered, powering the transport. A quick rib-squeeze later and we were back in solitary with the sleeping baby lawyer.

"Here's the deal." I rounded on Jean. "You remember that confusion charm I used on your brother Dominique a while back?" Jean's half-brother hated me, and he'd deserved that charm.

"He was quite addled," Jean said. "*Pourquoi?*"

"Because I have another one right here"—I patted my chest, a movement he tracked closely—"and I will not hesitate to use it on you if you don't do everything I say. You'll be totally at my mercy. I can make you dance and sing naked in front of your fellow inmates with just a suggestion and you will not be able to refuse me. Do you understand?"

I got the stony look. Jean hated nothing more than being under someone else's control or being humiliated. "Very well, Drusilla, but we must discuss your inappropriate behavior once we are home."

Whatever.

I leaned over and poked Mick with the elven staff. "Mick—wake up!"

He groaned and opened his eyes. Closed them again and began to snore. Damn it. He wasn't going to wake up enough to help. "Let's get him undressed," I told Jean, tugging off Mick's shoes. "You're going to wear this suit."

Time to see what we could do with Officer Jones.

Thirteen

FOLLOWING THE OFFICER'S INSTRUCTIONS, I knocked three times on the door and stepped back, the largest of the confusion charms clutched in my right hand. He was a very big guy and I wanted him to be very confused.

"When he opens the door, stand out of sight and wait for me to throw the charm," I told Jean. "Then slip around him and make sure there's no one else outside. Got it?"

"*Oui.*"

Keys rattled at the door, and I stood back far enough to hit Officer Jones with the charm as soon as I had a clear view of his face. Charms worked better with a facial assault, where the fumes would have a straight shot to the brain.

The door swung open and Officer Jones looked down at me with a frown. Then his gaze shifted to the bunk, where poor Mick, now dressed in the prison jumpsuit, lay curled on his side with a pillow covering his hair.

"What's going on? Where's the lawyer who—"

I thumbed off the top of the vial and tossed the full contents into the officer's face. Some of it even appeared to go up his nose since I was throwing from a height disadvantage. Jackpot.

"What the hell?" He stepped into the room, then stopped. He looked around in confusion. His pupils dilated to the size of dinner plates, and he looked down at me with a goofy smile. "Hello, my name is Jeff."

"Hi, Jeff. I'm DJ and this is Mick, the attorney."

Jean, who'd squeezed himself into Mick's suit and tied his hair back with my ponytail band, nodded to Jeff as he sidled past to check the hallway.

"Jeff, we need you to do us a favor. Can you do that?"

The officer blinked and wiped away a few tears. I wasn't sure if he was crying out of confusion or because some of the charm had gotten into his eyes. "Can I?"

"Yes, you can." Damn, that was a good charm. I should use it more often. It wore off in a few hours and had no lingering effects. "Mick has another legal client who is being interrogated. Could you help us find him so he can have his lawyer present?"

"I think I can call someone and find out where he is." Jeff paused. "Is that right?"

"No, you can't call because the phones aren't working. You'll have to take us to where the interrogation rooms are located. If anyone asks what you're doing, you'll tell them you're escorting a suspect's lawyer to him. Do you understand?"

"I'm escorting a suspect's lawyer." Jeff nodded.

"The way is clear, *Jolie.*" Jean reappeared behind the officer. "We should not tarry."

Right, no tarrying. "Take us to the interrogation rooms now, Jeff," I said.

"I'll take you now."

I closed the door behind us, locking poor Mick in the cell. He would have a raging headache and a lot of explaining he couldn't do when he woke up.

Jeff ambled down the hallway slower than a gator headed for the sausage factory. We'd never get there at this rate.

"Jeff, there is a fire in the interrogation rooms and you are the only one who can help. We must hurry."

"There is a fire," he said, breaking into a loping run. Even Jean had trouble keeping up with him, and the pirate reached back to grab my hand and drag me along behind.

We rushed back through the lobby area so fast that if anyone had done a double-take, they'd have thought they hallucinated the whole thing—the goofy running officer, the man in a ponytail wearing an ill-fitting pinstripe suit, and the short blonde being dragged behind, wielding a two-foot stick of wood.

We raced to another hallway, where Officer Jeff stopped so abruptly that we ran into him.

"What's wrong, Jeff?" I struggled to get the words out between gasps for breath. I ran at least three mornings a week. I should be in better shape than this.

"I don't know where the fire is. Where is the fire?"

"Let's see if we can find it." I began trying doors. The first three were locked, but the fourth swung open, revealing a sullen merman facing me and the cop from the parking lot, who swiveled in his chair at the interruption. I wasn't sure which of the two looked more surprised.

The officer looked past me and spotted Jeff. "Hey Jones, what're you doing here? I'm trying to interrogate a suspect."

"There is a fire." Jeff pushed past me into the room, looking in the corners and under the table. "Where is the fire? I have to put it out."

"Man, there ain't no fire in here. What's wrong with—"

While Jeff had been searching for the fire, I'd dug out another sleep charm and now doused the interrogator with it. His head hit the table with a crack.

Jeff leaned over and studied his fellow officer's face. "Why is Leonard sleeping? Is he on fire? Is that man your client?"

"Yes, Monsieur Jeff, he is my client," Jean said.

I closed the door to the hallway before any of this lunacy could be overheard. "Rene, let Officer Jeff sit in your chair."

"No problem, babe." He got up and stood alongside Jean.

"Jeff, would you sit down here? You're very tired."

Jeff sat in the chair facing his snoring fellow officer. "Leonard is tired too."

"He sure is." I dug one last sleeping charm out of my bra, flipped open the vial, and tossed the contents in Jeff's face. He went from confusion to unconscious in less time than I could say *pirate ship*.

The table took up most of the space in the tiny interrogation room, so I shooed Jean and Rene out of my way and made a transport in what little real estate I had left.

I talked as I worked. "We're going to transport to Rene's pickup. As soon as we get there, jump out of the back and get in the truck. Wait for me. Then I'm gonna transport the whole thing to Barataria."

"I don't want my truck in the Beyond. It messed with my transmission the one time I tried it." Rene's face turned mulish.

"Too bad. Do what I say or I'll hit you with a confusion charm too."

"That wizard needs an attitude adjustment," Rene said to Jean.

"*Oui*, I have discussed this with her already. She has grown most willful and demanding. A woman's tantrums should not be indulged."

I laid down the last bit of salt and pointed my staff at them. "Indulge this. Now get in the transport."

The three of us could barely squeeze inside it. "Jean pull in your foot, or you'll end up in Barataria a one-footed pirate. Privateer. Whatever."

"*Mon Dieu*, Drusilla. You are being most disagreeable."

Once the offending foot was inside the transport, I knelt and touched Charlie to the salt. "Rene's truck."

Another uncomfortable compression, and we materialized in the back of the truck, causing a woman in a blue Honda

Civic to crash into a sheriff's office patrol car when she saw us.

"In the pickup. *Now.*" I held up the last confusion charm, and my grumbling escapees got in the truck. "And don't even think about leaving me here."

I paced off the fastest transport in history using the last of my iron filings—I wasn't sure salt was strong enough to power the transport of an extended-cab pickup jacked up on big tires. Then I stopped.

My brilliant plan had one flaw. I wouldn't be able to power the transport from inside the truck. Couldn't anything be simple?

Apparently not. I stepped on the driver's side running board, held onto the door handle, and leaned down with Charlie to touch the transport. "Old Barataria," I said, then flipped a bird at Rene grinning through the truck window.

Sometime during the suck of the transport, I lost hold of the pickup's door handle and landed on a rotten wooden surface, facedown. At least I still had the staff. From the corner of my eye, I spotted the pickup perched atop what was left of *Le Diligent's* navigation deck, or whatever they called them back in the olden days. The scene was illuminated by several flambeaux that had been set up around the transport, and the full moon shone overhead. Back in the Beyond.

I sat up, picking splinters out of my sweater and yawning. Something wet dribbled down my chest, and I looked down the inside front of my sweater. I'd just registered the smell of a broken vial of a sleep charm when a wave of dizziness hit me.

Jean and Rene already were out of the truck and on their hands and knees around the area where, I assumed, they thought the gold might be.

"Don't mind me," I said, yawning again. "I'm just gonna head on home." I was going to talk to Alex and tell him everything. Sometime during the prison break, it hit me that I really missed him. I'd been wrong to go on this trip without telling him. I vowed to do better, to make things work. Maybe I'd never ask his permission to do what I thought was right, but I also wouldn't hide things from him.

"Go on home. See ya later, babe." The upper half of Rene's body disappeared into a hole in the rotting wood as he leaned in to look around. Jean pulled off Mick's suit coat and shirt and studied the wound on his chest, which looked worse than ever.

"I'm going home to sleep now." I struggled to my feet and half walked, half fell off the edge of *Le Diligent* and onto the muddy ground of Grand Terre Island. "I'll just make a new transport."

"Farewell, *Jolie.*" Jean, now back on his hands and knees, never looked up. "What find you, Rene?"

"Got it!" Rene's hand reappeared out of the hole, several gold coins clutched in his fingers.

"I could use some gold," I said. My house had few walls and no heat.

They ignored me, intent upon dumping gold coins on the deck. One rolled off and landed near my feet, in a patch of mud. I dug it out, still yawning, and stuffed it in my pocket. The sleep charm was taking hold.

"Bye, guys. I'm off."

I might have heard a muffled goodbye from inside *Le Diligent*, but it might have been my imagination. Under the light of the full moon, I walked down the hill to the narrow stretch of beach, scratched out a transport in the sand, and touched the staff to its edge.

Finally, I would get some sleep.

About the Author

Suzanne Johnson is the author of the Sentinels of New Orleans urban fantasy series for Tor Books, including the 2014 Gayle Wilson Award-winning *Elysian Fields*. Book five in the series, Belle Chasse, will be released by Tor in November 2016.

Writing as Susannah Sandlin, she is author of the Penton Legacy paranormal romance series for Montlake Romance, including the 2013 Holt Medallion winner for paranormal romance *Absolution*, as well as The Collectors romantic suspense series, including *Lovely, Dark, and Deep*, 2015 Holt Medallion winner and 2015 Booksellers Best Award winner for romantic suspense. Her new Louisiana-based Wildlife Wardens romantic suspense series kicks off in spring 2016 with *Wild Man's Bluff.*

A displaced New Orleanian, Suzanne currently lives in Auburn, Alabama, where she is editor of the quarterly *Auburn Magazine* at Auburn University. Since she attended the University of Alabama, she claims to be bilingual and can say "War Eagle" and "Roll Tide" in the same sentence with a straight face. Suzanne loves SEC football, crawfish bread, all things New Orleans (including a certain undead French pirate and Cajun merman), and redneck reality TV.

For more information, please visit Suzanne's website:
www.suzannejohnsonauthor.com

Click on the newsletter tab and subscribe for monthly updates, release news, sneak peeks and special giveaways:
www.suzannejohnsonauthor.com/newsletter.
www.facebook.com/AuthorSuzanneJohnson
www.twitter.com/Suzanne_Johnson